LOST IN THE CITY OF LIGHT

LOST IN THE
CITY OF LIGHT

. . . .

Richard de Combray

ALFRED A. KNOPF   NEW YORK

1 9 8 9

THIS IS A BORZOI BOOK
PUBLISHED BY ALFRED A. KNOPF, INC.

Grateful acknowledgment is made to the following for permission to reprint previously published material:

Doubleday Publishing: Excerpts from *The Odyssey* by Homer, translated by Robert Fitzgerald. Copyright © 1961 by Robert Fitzgerald. Reprinted by permission of Doubleday.

The Putnam Publishing Group: Excerpt from "The Golden Ball" by Agatha Christie. Copyright 1924 by Agatha Christie. Reprinted by permission of The Putnam Publishing Group.

Random House, Inc.: Excerpt from "Song X" from *Collected Poems* by W. H. Auden. Copyright 1950 by W. H. Auden. Reprinted by permission of Random House, Inc.

Library of Congress Cataloging-in-Publication Data
De Combray, Richard.
Lost in the city of light / Richard de Combray.—1st ed.
p. cm.
ISBN 0-394-57754-X
PS3554.E11147L6 1989
I. Title.
813'.54—dc19   89-2540 CIP

Manufactured in the United States of America
First Edition

· · · · · ·

FOR

ROBERT FERRO

AND

MICHAEL GRUMLEY

· · · · · ·

There stands the deserted castle
Ready to explore;
Enter, climb the marble staircase
Open the locked door

Cross the silent empty ballroom,
Doubt and danger past;
Blow the cobwebs from the mirror
See yourself at last.

W . H . A U D E N , *Song X*

LOST IN THE CITY OF LIGHT

1

. . . . . .

A n American in Paris is not necessarily Gene Kelly dancing through the streets of Montmartre. This is what Kevin Korlov (American) thought as he walked home muffled inside his scarf, his woolens, his Burberry raincoat. In a lacerating wind he turned into his doorway on the rue St. Placide, not far from the corner of the rue de Rennes where one of the terrorist bombs was recently tossed, killing and maiming passersby and tearing a hole in the flesh of the city.

He pushed the code that opened the carved door leading to his building. By Parisian standards it was an ordinary apartment house, though its door was monumental. This was the thing about Paris, thought Kevin as he headed toward the stairway: incredible refinements masking mediocrity. And the reverse. He ought to have known. Fortune, playing its usual tricks, had pitched him in Paris a half-dozen years ago, just as he'd hit thirty and was trying to be a sculptor. How easy it had seemed then. A visiting French gallery owner named Dryfuss, seeing his work in a competition at New York's Pratt Institute, had said, "That work by what's-his-name, the one who did the lame bronze saint and that bust of Edith Wharton. His things will fit in nicely mid-March, just after the big Cremonini show,'' turning his attention elsewhere.

The two sentences must have set something of a record for altering a man's destiny. Which Kevin hadn't even heard.

A fluke, foisted on him by unexpected circumstance. A future reserved for someone else. Time had blunted the edges of the show's disappointment (he sold three bronzes, all told) but with prudent managing of his funds Kevin decided that he could survive in Paris for a while. Paris, meanwhile, claimed another foreign resident to its cold, colossal breast.

Now coming toward him was the concierge, a large woman from a newly hewn equatorial republic who was given to making exotic, voodoo statements. She wore immense, beltless garments in African hues. A letter was swinging from between the tips of her fingers.

''This was put in my hand. By a tall lady. And then she went into the taxicab awaiting. She wore no perfume.''

Kevin took the letter and muttered his thanks. He was not feeling communicative, having gotten out of bed before six when it was black outside and 4 degrees centigrade. One of the many jobs he'd found to pay his rent et cetera, was a once-a-week radio broadcast in English, at Radio Arc de Triomphe. This week's program, beamed to America and meant to entertain persons of French descent or inclination, was ''Frenchmen of Letters: Who Now?''

He did not like the feel of the envelope. The glue on the back of it seemed to be still moist. Its content was too fresh. Why was the concierge standing there as though expecting to be read to?

''I hope the news it good,'' she called after him. ''The gentleman on the first floor received just this morning a big bunch of roses. Mixed colors. White and pink.''

''Thank you, thank you,'' Kevin repeated over his shoulder, his steps dragging a bit as he climbed. Already ill-tempered, he did not need to hear any more about the dashing rogue on the first floor.

"Okay, okay, take it easy," he said as he unbolted his door. A small, elderly dog, The General, scuttled toward him and began performing a creaky though elaborate reception ritual. Kevin patted the dog and then turned his attention to the letter, though the one-dog entertainment produced for his benefit alone continued with undiminishing fervor at his feet.

"Kevin, dear Kevin," it read in a majestic backhand. "We are finished. I do not mean to be blunt. But I am empty when we are together. My teaching work in Lyons is so pedagogical that when I am finished and take my train each week to Paris I need more fun. FUN! All day long I sit next to my pupils as they run up and down the scales or attempt to play "Für Elise." Oh, God! When I leave them I want Liszt! Scriabin! Not some diddle, diddle, diddle on the keyboard of Life itself.

"I cannot be with you anymore in the flesh. Spiritually I shall always be there, and I am leaving you The General to prove it to you. He likes it here better than back and forth on the train to Lyons. And I know you love him. He will be an inspiration to you as he has been to me. He is my gift to you. So that's it, I guess. Bye bye, Beatrice."

Kevin folded the letter back into its envelope. "Good riddance," he said aloud. Looking down at the wire-haired dachshund who now lay on its back, paws spinning like propellers, he added, "Christ, what am I going to do with you?"

Now that his horizon stretched ahead Beatrice-less, Kevin had to assess his new situation. In the past four months the Piano Teacher (which is how he intended to refer to her from now on) had spent a few nights a week in his apartment. Then she'd rush back to Lyons to give her lessons, leaving him the dog. True, he had become rather fond of the scraggly creature. As for Beatrice, her main charm, he now told himself, was her superior length. When wrapped together on those cold, miserably heated nights, they warmed each other nicely from head to toe. In addition, there was their mutual, passionate interest in classical music. It was a relationship. It was better than being alone. It was pathetic, really. A wintertime affair.

Kevin sat at his desk, trying to concentrate on the high pile of notebooks in front of him. Another of his jobs was teaching ambitious young French students at the Worldwide Language Center the pleasures and torments of the English language. As an exercise he had asked them to describe as best they could some of their fantasies about visiting America. Red pencil poised, he stared down at an opened page. ". . . and I am expecting also that I will discover sweetshirts and jeans," he read, "for under two hundred francs, also leather cowboy boots, these ones with metal points on their tips." He closed the book and tilted back in his chair, idly wishing that spring would arrive.

As if that would make any difference. But it was February; his very bones felt cold and his heart as well. Maybe weather was unnaturally important to him, he had to admit, because he was so much alone. His few girlfriends had behaved more or less like Beatrice, though none of them had left him with a beat-up dachshund. He gamely tried to muster up some positives. Luckily, he had his sculpture to concentrate on. This he knew was a lie.

As it was only just ten in the morning, and as the day was unfolding unpleasantly and without a plan, Kevin decided that he must in all conscience visit the unheated studio he'd rented years ago for what he thought of as his real work, his sculpting. But in time the long Métro ride out to the Porte des Lilas had become a self-inflicted misery, for nothing much came of it other than periodic bouts of the flu. Weeks had gone by since he was last there. He closed his eyes and pictured the small, shrouded bronzes, unsold, standing around on homemade pedestals.

"I've got to give it a try," he said as he lifted the pensioned General from his lap, grabbed his coat, his hat, his woolen muffler, and with grim resolve readied himself to battle the cold streets once again. The bulky Mrs. Bomwalla had again taken up her watch near the front door, though pretending to read a heavily illustrated woman's magazine.

"Not bad news, I hope? Bad news comes quicker than good news. That lady who left the envelope was so rushed, so tall. She tripped on the way out. When women trip, their mind is somewhere else. We have a saying that when a person trips too much he has intentions to be on another road." She then giggled, slapping her lap with her magazine. She looked like a bundle of African laundry.

Then Kevin laughed too, cheered on by Mrs. Bomwalla. "We have a saying, too," he shot back over his shoulder as he pushed open the massive door. "The road to hell is paved like any other road." He rushed through the street, fumbling in his pocket for Beatrice's note—which he'd brought with him to reread, intending to fan the fire of his anger—and threw it into a wire trash bin before going down the steps of the Métro.

The building near the Porte des Lilas trembled with Arab music. From all the thin doors lining the corridors it wailed and beat at the walls in accompaniment to many mamas screaming bilingually, their kids bouncing and squabbling on their cots inside. The air was filled with the spicy scent of merguez sausages frying on the two-burner stoves. None of this bothered Kevin, who saw in it an inspiring connection to *La Bohème,* updated. He nodded to an Algerian gentleman making his way hastily to the toilet at the end of the hall.

"Cold, cold," said the man. *"Un froid de canard.* My kidneys are in ruin." There was no time to reply. As usual, Kevin's key jammed in the door; he twisted it, kicked at the door, heaved himself against it. Now he was inside the squalid, sanctified area he referred to as his work space. His routine never varied. He would light the gas stove, rub his hands together, remind himself that he was an artist in Paris, and begin working in the chill on the molded wax that would eventually become—via the lost-wax method—a bronze sculpture. But he knew he did not have the temperament to sell the stuff anyway, or to grab the attention of the art galleries, or hustle the collectors. He knew this—deeply knew it—but was not prepared to surrender the label, which was how he defined himself in public. He was still Kevin-the-Artist. And he was still paying rent on the place.

So bereft was he of ideas that over a month ago he had begun on a self-portrait, and now he sat on a high wooden stool, a dusty mirror opposite him, his incompleted work adjacent, tools in hand, and stared hard at his reflection. His own real face, he felt, had been sculpted without affection. A face lacking any significant planes and ridges, those familiar signposts with which we are able to distinguish beauty and dreadfulness, and almost all the possibilities in between. The eyes surely had an intelligent sparkle, but they were framed and somewhat obscured by horn-rimmed glasses of some bland, translucent plastic. A beard, perhaps? A mustache? Kevin had considered these, but his beard grew at a tediously slow rate and lacked that density marking a serious beard. The mustache, when he tried it out, was too spare. In short, his face was marked by an absence of anything to distinguish it. Which he well knew and had made peace with. I am not all that bad-looking, is how he put it.

He remained there until the day darkened toward three-thirty, listening to the Three-Part Inventions on his small cassette player. As though in concert with Glenn Gould he frowned, he hummed, he muttered, his face, its reflection, and the work in front of him alternately repelling and soothing him into a kind of stupor. When his concentration lagged, he got up, stretched, and walked to the window to look at the electrician bent over his table in the shop across the street. These were the dangerous moments, when he would ask himself whether his work was even as important as wiring a brass fitting. What would he do with this piece of sculpture when it was finished? Donate it to the city of Paris? Send it to his aunt in West Hartford?

On his way home to the rue St. Placide Kevin stopped at the supermarket. There he had the opportunity to gaze upon the pretty, unsmiling checkout cashier who occupied a small niche in his erotic gallery. She wordlessly took his money and handed him his change. She possessed no charm, no sense of charity. Her main pleasure seemed to come from waiting for her customers to plead for a slippery plastic bag stamped Codex in which they might put their purchases.

"It's certainly cold today," he ventured. "A real *froid de canard.*"

"Ummm."

Her petulant lips glistened, her eyes glazed, she waited while Kevin's fingers fumbled as he tried to separate the sides of the bag so that he could fill it. Then she pushed a hidden button with her knee and the conveyor belt started. She turned back to her cash register, and readied her negative responses as her day spun wearily on.

It's those lips, thought Kevin later as he unpacked his groceries, imagining someone ripping off her pale blue Supermarché Codex smock and dragging her toward the table where the vegetables lay, pinning her down against the radishes, red as those glistening lips.

"I'm alone too much," he said aloud, leaning over to place a carton of milk on the refrigerator door. The cold, cold interior reserved comment.

"I haven't decided whether or not you stay, so don't get too attached," he said to the dog. He then bent down and spooned a small can of Pal into a ceramic dish. The small dachshund turned its back to Kevin and the food and left the kitchen.

Kevin hacked at some butter and threw it into a frying pan, leaving it to melt on too high a flame while he washed the leeks, removed one or two of their outer layers, and sliced off their leathery tops. He saw the plume of smoke rising from the top of the stove just in time to save the butter from sizzling and turning brown. He placed six neat cubes of veal (three for tomorrow's lunch) into a casserole and opened a tin of carrots and peas, removed from the refrigerator some potatoes he had cooked the previous evening, and realized that he'd forgotten to buy the onions. The phone rang, shattering his accumulating despair.

"I am probably the only friend you have who can remember when the telephone exchanges in Paris had names like Jasmin, or Trocadéro, or Elysée. Mine, when I lived here in 'fifty-three, was Babylone 2499. I can recall it to this day. Their replacement by eight, cold digits has not polished the luster of France."

"Sasha! I'd know that accent of yours anywhere."

"Well, I am inviting you to dinner. I know how you starving artists are always happy to put on a tie now and then. Shall we say Le Grand Véfour at eight?"

"Wait a minute. What are you doing in Paris?"

"Buying works of art to sell to the gentry of Beverly Hills. Can you hold on a minute?" Not quite covering the mouthpiece he began a rapid conversation in German while Kevin's eyes swept across the casserole and the leeks.

"I must go now," Sasha continued, turning his attention back to Kevin. "I now have to see a man about a small metal plaque by Mucha, not unlike the celebrated portrait of Sarah Bernhardt. Le Grand Véfour at eight?"

"You didn't ask me whether I was busy," said Kevin.

There was a pause. "That's what I like about you. Your sense of realism. Given that it is February, and miserable, and that Paris is not the most congenial city in the world, I thought there was a good chance you might be free."

"Well, you're right."

"So that's settled." Sasha hung up.

As a starving artist, the usual drill was that Kevin would be lured out for an expensive dinner paid for by an expense account, and while wolfing down all that rich food, stuffing his digestive system beyond reason, he would realize that his dazed, equally burdened mind was getting squeezed dry for information about what was happening in Paris—what discos, what restaurants (for other meals, other guests), what exhibitions, operas, ballets, monuments, museums, shops, trips—and what about what's happening in other cities like London and Milan? However, with Sasha Wittenburg this was not the case. Sasha belonged to that race of international people whose barbers never err, whose tailors see to it that their ever expanding waistlines never offend. He could talk on any subject and was at ease everywhere. It was Wittenburg who had bought the bronze of the lamed saint from the gallery on the rue des Beaux Arts, asking to meet the artist. Throughout the years they had managed to see each other only a half-dozen times, for Wittenburg was a busy man.

Now that there was time before dressing for dinner, Kevin thought of calling the Piano Teacher in Lyons to tell her a few disagreeable things. But instead, he sat in his favorite chair, crossed his long legs, and opened a book, a collection of Agatha Christie stories. He read them like myths or fables; something in him always longed for stories with happy endings.

He read:

> A scarlet touring car with an immense long hood had drawn up to the curb beside him. At the wheel was that beautiful and popular society girl, Mary Montresor . . . She was smiling at George in an accomplished manner.
>
> "I never knew a man could look so like an island," said Mary Montresor. "Would you like to get in?"
>
> "I should love it above all things," said George with no hesitation, and stepped in beside her.
>
> They proceeded slowly because the traffic forbade anything else.

"I should love it above all things," said Kevin aloud as he stood now shaving before the bathroom mirror. He had a good voice, which is why he earned money at Radio Arc de Triomphe. A sinus specialist once told Kevin that he had the largest antrums he had ever come upon; causing the voice to reverberate strongly against their wider than average walls. It was in a voice now geared to oratory that Kevin again repeated, "I should love it above all things," trying it out just in case the situation arose, standing, say, on the Place Vendôme, not far from the Ritz, waiting to cross the street as a long car came cruising around the corner of the rue de la Paix. He pictured the car, a deep maroon convertible; and the woman, of course, would be blond, Carole Lombard, her hair swept sidewise by the breeze as she leaned toward him, her foot on the brake, the motor idling. Blue eyes sparkling with wit, she would look him straight in the eye. There would be laughter in the sound of her voice as she said, "I never knew a man could look so much like an island."

He rinsed the razor and placed it neatly into the glass next to the toothbrush. Then he brought his hairbrush very gently across the thinning hairs covering the top of his head. In an exercise dredged up from a yoga course taken at the YMCA back in the seventies, he closed his eyes and stood at the washbasin rocking gently on his heels. It was only a moment but it calmed him.

The General, standing there at attention, watched these private ablutions and rituals. His presence was a continuing reproach, a confirmation of Kevin's solitude. But he hadn't needed the dog around to remind him. In fact, he had always been considered a loner, even back in the States when he was growing up. He tried to take his portions of solitude respectfully, like a prescribed drug, for along with food and water this solitude had become one of the essential, inescapable elements in his life.

"Listen, kid," he said, trying not to be charmed by the attentiveness, the concern, the alertness with which the animal was watching every move. "This isn't settled yet. When your mama gets back we'll see whether you can find another home. Leave it to her to wait until you're so old that . . . Well, it shouldn't take her long to land another dogsitter." He leaned down to run his fingers through the dog's curly, thinning fur.

After carefully dressing for dinner, Kevin pushed the *minuterie* that illuminated the stairway for precisely three minutes, clattering down the steps for the third time that day as Paris prepared for its long winter evening. No stars appeared in the wintry sky that stretched above, toward the Bastille, toward Strasbourg, Nuremberg, Prague, and Krakow, where at this hour scant generations ago, earlier Korlovs had already begun to retire for the night, glancing out at the cold cobbled streets, wondering whether they would ever manage to get themselves on a boat that would take them to the golden shores of America.

2

· · · · · ·

The Palais-Royal was eerily quiet. Kevin entered through the one open gate and walked along, his newly heeled and best pair of loafers echoing throughout the long open corridor, The General hurrying along as best he could, long black toenails clicking like castanets. Walking past the regiment of lanterns they made a curious couple, casting behind them wildly unequal shadows across the dark, noble arcades that always made Kevin think of the Piazza San Marco. This is where the revolution was announced, he thought, this is where Charlotte Corday bought the knife that cut Marat's throat. But at the far end of the gardens, where he anticipated a warming cube of light emanating from Le Grand Véfour, was darkness.

"Kevin?" The call came from a very large rented Mercedes parked at the curb on the rue de Beaujolais. "It's colder than a witch's whatnot out there," said Sasha from within, the window open just enough to allow his voice to penetrate the silent street. "Get yourself inside before we both freeze to death."

Kevin obliged, easing himself into the cushioned warmth

of the car. "Closed on Thursdays," he said. "I forgot about that." Not that he ever knew.

"As did I," said Sasha. "The concierge insisted that I try another place. He was certain that I'd love it. Now, the last time I saw you, you were teaching English and speaking on the radio. I still have your saint, as I remind you every year, on its pedestal in the foyer."

Kevin produced a smile that was almost wistful. "Here I am, very much the way I was a year ago, and the year before that."

"It seems to me that you uprooted yourself by coming to live in Paris. And having made the gesture you feel you've never got yourself properly transplanted. It's a horticultural problem."

"I guess you could say that."

Sasha turned away with a world-weary sigh. "Yes, this is a frequent problem foreigners have in Europe. Here, in Rome, in Spain . . ." He gestured vaguely, his meticulously manicured nails briefly glinting in the passing light. "When I left Vienna at the beginning of the war I knew that I would inevitably become a permanent exile. But it suited me. It's always different when Europeans embed themselves in the soil of America."

"Nice to see you, Sasha," said Kevin.

"Well, nice to see you, too." He smiled broadly. "I like to keep up with you, to see how you are getting along. But these last few times I admit that I've been bewildered. When you first came here you seemed so full of wonder. It was a nice quality, one that I admire."

"I still am. The beauty of the place still amazes me."

"I seem to remember that well into one's thirties one has a very serious decision to make about where it is all leading, simply because the road ahead is far shorter than one had previously believed. But who am I to say what to do about it? In a way I find myself with fewer and fewer solutions, simply because I can see too many points of view." He paused, preparing the kind of one-liner his friends would quote. "I miss the clarity of the uninformed," he said with satisfaction.

"Well, I'd appreciate any of your directions, of course."

Sasha looked ahead, his large profile that of a doge administering justice. "I can only tell you to slightly exceed the speed limit," he said. "Now, who is this venerable, droll character with these bushy eyebrows who's joining us at the restaurant for dinner—the French are so welcoming when it comes to animals—a *teckel à poil dur?* Ah, yes, far more appealing than the ordinary dachshund, shorter nose and body, something like that Wizard of Oz dog. I bet you've got a fine pedigree." He reached over and offered the dog a few light taps, received without comment by The General whose nose—still rather long by ordinary standards—remained fixed at the window.

"A veteran of many campaigns," said Kevin. "A portable pal."

"Oh, we've got to do better than *that* for you," said Sasha Wittenburg in a voice that resounded with experience in manipulating the lives of others.

At one of the preferred tables of Le Bourdonnais Kevin sliced into his little *mignons* of veal, past the lemon slices and through the web of crisscrossed orange rind. He said, "I didn't expect nouvelle cuisine."

"Nor did I. Well, we're here, so make the best of it. I worry when I hear my friends saying that so many things have deteriorated in the name of progress. I refuse. It is the obvious trap of middle age to find oneself saying how wonderful things were."

"I'm thirty-six, and I began complaining at about eight, so you're talking to the wrong person. I tend to be suspicious of new things."

"Not I, not I," boasted Sasha. "I try to keep up with the times. I am thinking of dealing in computer art. Amazing things. Disposable, perhaps, but in America these are disposable times."

"Ah, yes. That is true. That's why living here is such a continuing pleasure." A fatuous remark, if ever he had heard one, that Wittenburg magnanimously overlooked.

They proceeded to the next course, and the next, and the next. The *crevettes purée de Noailles* had given way to the *filets mignons de veau au citron;* then arrived the *petites aubergines hachées aux raisins de Palerme,* which was succeeded by a reasonably intelligible lemon soufflé; the white wine had given way to a red and now a Sauternes. Kevin had unnotched his belt and was breathing more heavily. He did not take too well to alcohol.

"You know what I was saying before?" Sasha leaned across the table to remark, sotto voce, "about computers? It astonishes me how they are used here for all kinds of vices. Quite delicious. The vices, I mean, not the soufflé."

Kevin had been spooning it all in, not caring any longer whether it combined with the rest, or that the truffled chocolate cakes with crème fraîche still to come would finish him off. "I can hardly imagine you interested in what you call vices," Kevin managed to say.

"Oh, you misjudge me! Just because I seem to you—if I may say so—a rather urbane gentleman does not mean that I don't qualify for my share of fun and games! And the French have one-upped the Americans this time." Sasha paused for emphasis, and to reassure himself that he was not speaking into the void. Kevin was looking quite pale.

"And what's that?"

"The Minitel! Fan*tas*tic. I mean fan*tas*tic." Sasha put down his fork to dramatize.

"That television computer thing you hook up to your phone?"

"Precisely! If I had the connections I'd buy the copyright. Outright. And sell them in America. They'd bring in a lot more income than the genteel objects I now sell. They've produced a million and a half of them here, loaned them out—they cost the phone company three hundred dollars each—*loaned* them out so that the public will get hooked on them. Like the hotels in Las Vegas that leave five silver dollars in your room when you check in, just to lure you to the gaming tables downstairs. Here, Mr. John Q. Pub*lique* installs the Minitel, dials in a code, and on the screen he can acquire airline information, order his tickets, get stock prices, the latest news, find out what cattle is selling for—the machine is a miracle. And best of all—"

"I've got one," said Kevin to assure his friend that he was following along. "My bank gave me one. I used it once to check on my balance. When you hook into it, it costs something like fifty cents for two minutes."

"Exactly! The phone company keeps half of it, and the other half goes to the man who operates whatever service you tap into. There are franchises for new services opening every day! Fortunes are paid for them, because the whole country's gone Minitel mad. And best of all—"

"I used mine once in six months," continued Kevin, worried about a sour taste filling his mouth.

"—are those little so-called message services. That's where the money is!"

"*Message* services? Is that what all those posters are about? Half-naked girls, half-naked boys advertising 'Dial whatever and love comes into your life'? I can't imagine anyone taking it seriously. You least of all."

"Well, Kevin, I used one last night." Sasha's large lips suddenly looked even larger as he mouthed his words in a near whisper. "The concierge very politely sent a Minitel to my room and hooked it up to my phone. Don't tell me you've never done this. For heaven's sake," he hissed, "you *live* here!"

Kevin, too stuffed to speak, simply shook his head. "Just coffee," he said, looking up at the arriving waiter. "A great deal of coffee."

"I will have the truffled chocolate cake, and also some coffee," announced Sasha. He patted his stomach. "And a dish of water for The General." To himself he added, "I hope I've remembered to bring my Sweet-n-Low. Now, what was I saying. Ah yes!" He continued. "I hadn't planned on discussing this, but after all"—he again slapped expansively at the vest covering his wide waist—"why not? I guess the old story is true: it takes someone from out of town. Rather like showing a New Yorker the Statue of Liberty. Well, you dial in a message service like the ones you've seen advertised. The bellboy who brought the machine to my room told me to type G-I-L-D-A. GILDA. Then you hang up the phone and watch the Minitel. Like magic, on the screen appears a computerized drawing of a pair of lips, and between them a blank space where you type in what they call a *pseudo,* which, of course, is your pseudonym for yourself. Or, more interestingly, your fantasy of yourself."

"And you?" Kevin asked, finally intrigued. "You wrote CALIFORNIA ART DEALER, right?"

Sasha sighed with exasperation. "I wrote," he said, "VISITING STUD."

"Whoa!" said Kevin, in spite of himself.

"Then a list appears—your pseudo is one of, say, eighty—and there are all these boys and girls, men and women, all over Paris—all over France!—hoping to make contact with each other. Someone likes my pseudo, VISITING STUD, and writes me a message on the screen. And perhaps I write a message to BLACK LACE NIGHTIE. You've no reason to appear so shocked. Ought I to stop recounting this?''

"No!" said Kevin. "I wasn't shocked, just unprepared."

Sasha's enthusiasm had now begun to pale. "I know of no other way to tell it to you," he said, eyeing the dessert.

"I think you're trying to shake me up."

"Yes, I think you are right. Now if you'd like, we can discuss Art."

"Oh, *no!*" said Kevin.

"Oh, yes," said Sasha, putting his fork into the truffled chocolate.

3

· · · · · · ·

GILDA. You just dial a telephone number (3615), fill in the name of the service you want, and a computerized pair of lips appears on the screen of the Minitel connected to it. How simple it all sounded, how effortless, how mysterious, to sit back and make someone's acquaintance by way of a machine.

Dizzied and still sick, Kevin managed to get himself inside the door before beating a hasty retreat down the narrow, underheated corridor into his bathroom where he bathed his face in cold water. He slowly removed his clothing—which he hung up and did not simply leave strewn about on the floor—and lay on his bed, weakened, feeling considerably better and unexpectedly righteous. Sasha Wittenburg indeed. Man of the world, with signed photographs in silver frames (he was imagining this) of Queen Elizabeth, of Elizabeth Taylor, of . . . Well, it humanized Sasha to discover that he had his little vices. Incredibly, this gentleman twenty years his senior did not even have the grace to get the slightest bit sick from the ragbag of wines or that parade of designer food brought to the table and presented to the customers as though created by Oriental craftsmen.

Now he remembered a few nagging details. Once back in the Mercedes Sasha Wittenburg was just a bit aloof, as though tipsy Kevin had not been quite as amusing or responsive as he'd hoped. Not as much *fun,* as the Piano Teacher had pointed out. Was it possible that Wittenburg planned on telling his driver to go on to the Palace disco and other hotspots as soon as boring Kevin had been deposited on the rue St. Placide? "Jesus!" proclaimed Kevin to his pale bedroom walls, where faded haywagons were forever stranded in front of invincible Norman farmhouses: a repeat of seventeen patterns across and nine down which Kevin had, God help him, counted on the wallpaper one hideously solitary Sunday. Though that was a long time ago.

What a dreary business it was that he did not participate as expected, that he had allowed Paris to become simply a place where he put one foot in front of the other and kept moving. Paris! The word alone implied magical powers capable of changing lives. Plus all that erotic stuff. He looked down at his perfectly good body, then turned his head toward the unoccupied half of the bed where he detected on a dent in the pillow a small dog with wisps of graying fur, curled like a doughnut, snoring heavily.

Then and there, Kevin rose unsteadily from his bed. Vaguely he remembered reading about the Minitel in the latest issue of *Passion.* He bent over the cocktail table and drunkenly leafed through the magazine, turning clumps of pages at a time until he reached the article. Though now nude, he was still wearing his glasses.

"Originally launched in 1981 as a computerized alternative to conventional phone books . . ." He skimmed past the historical information searching for the sexier facts. "Nearly 4,000,000 little brown terminals (a tiny television screen and simple keyboard that hooks up to your phone at home or in the office) have been distributed . . . A wide variety of organizations, mail-order (now Minitel-order) businesses, magazines and other media have begun to produce Minitel versions of themselves. The charge of 98 centimes each minute. . . ." Blah blah blah. ". . . The services offered— over 3600(!!) and growing every day—include, among many others, these:" Kevin took a deep breath and tried to concentrate.

Agriculture, Banks, Sports Events, Airport, Train, Bus information, Cultural events, Animals, Tourism, Health, Law, Education, TV programs, Gardening, Stock quotations, Media information (news, etc.), Transports, Games, Gossip. AND HERE'S THE BEST PART!! The enormously successful *messageries*—programs that allow people across the country to meet and talk to each other over the screen. To hook yourself into this microchip madness, all you need is a Minitel terminal available free to telephone customers. Dial 3615 and wait for the high-pitched tone (more like a shriek). Press the button marked CONNEXION/FIN. Type in whatever service you wish, then press the ENVOI button. Put your feet up! Relax! Welcome to the Wonderful World of MINITEL!

There was no hesitation in what Kevin did next. He walked over to the Minitel, flicked the switch, dialed 3615 on the phone, heard a high-pitched sound (just as the article said, *more like a shriek),* and punched the connection button. CODE, it said. GILDA, he typed. COMMUNICATION ESTABLISHED, it said. Then, as promised, the miracle happened. An astonishing computer drawing of a large pair of lips gradually appeared line by line on the screen. YOUR PSEUDO? it asked, its cursor flickering impatiently where the lips parted.

Spellbound, Kevin sat there naked on his desk chair. What was his pseudonym? He started to type KEVIN, then changed his mind and pushed the correction button. The curser returned to the now empty space to throb beguilingly once more. YOUR PSEUDO? it repeated. VISITING STUD, he wrote, stared at it, and quickly canceled that, too. The flickering resumed impatiently. With a wrenching sense of defeat he watched himself reach firmly for the main switch to shut the machine off. His hand then hesitated for an instant in midair before joining its mate in his naked lap in what might have appeared, had anyone been around to notice, a combination of prayer and self-protection. Kevin stared at the blank screen as though waiting . . . waiting . . .

I seem to have spent my whole life waiting, he thought.

Was it all the alcohol he'd drunk that precipitated what followed? In a flash he was wrenching his clothes back on, grabbing his heavy coat out of the closet, and with it his brown plaid scarf, his woolen gloves, and even the hat that he wore because the thinning top of his head, God damn it, got cold. And ran down the stairs back into the ink-black night.

At the St. Placide station he caught the next-to-last Métro of the evening—it was just after midnight—boarding it without a destination. He scanned the list of station stops, deciding at random to go as far as the Gare du Nord. Visions flew at him of the chilled, dark cities, way above Paris: Antwerp, Utrecht, Bremen, Hamburg . . . all wrapped in the black, endless shroud of winter. There was a perfection about a northern train station in the dead of winter, the essence of the season's soul, the end of the line. Oh, perfect, perfect for this long evening.

Inside the Métro it was warm and empty. The car rolled along on its silent rubber wheels and only at Les Halles did it crowd up a little with groups of tired youths on their way home to the grimy suburbs where it was too late to hassle their parents, already in bed, wracked and defeated by reprimands both spoken and withheld. They chatted, they sang, they rubbed against one another. Disturbed by all the things he hadn't been, wasn't, and would never be, Kevin hurriedly left the Métro at his station.

Momentarily lost, the tiled labyrinth beneath the Gare du Nord pulled him in one direction and then another until he thought he'd been caught in a maze and could never get out. Finally a small staircase took him above, and he sped through the dark solemnity of the station, where no trains seemed to be going anywhere at that hour, emerging with relief onto the boulevard de Strasbourg. There the brasseries were just closing, the aproned shellfish vendors hauling in crates of oysters and *praires* and shoveling out the bins of shaved ice. Only when it occurred to him in brief split seconds did Kevin wonder what he was doing or where he was going, his idea only to keep in motion. And so he walked briskly down the empty, raw boulevards, past the sleeping clochards, oddly snug under their layering of blankets and rags, past the shuttered windows of the dimly lit hotels, turning toward the great stone arch, the Porte St. Denis, all sculpted palm trees, armor, and languishing lions, higher even than the Arc de Triomphe, built when this was the outermost margin of the city of Paris. Ah, yes, Paris. The city where fate had determined he would live. This brought a wry smile.

Passing beneath the arch, and, by holding his breath, trying to avoid the strong smell of urine, he turned abruptly into the street that slanted downward, toward the river. Which turned out to be the rue St. Denis, a brightly lit, bustling hornet's nest of whores.

Of course, he thought, I'd end up finding myself here.

Here the bitter cold was forgotten. Instead, the streets were alive with heated activity. Small agitated groups of men crossed and recrossed the rue St. Denis checking out the merchandise, or walked singly, with an air of resignation, behind their mobile purchases. Up the narrow, palely lit staircases they went, slouching on and on through the endless corridors of the hotels and rooming houses. The sidewalks in front were fringed with lines of unmatched girls. Girls: frilled girls, furred girls, fleecy girls; skin-tight spandex girls, stretchable leather-and-latex, sparkled-and-spangled miniskirted, high booted, low clogged, and spike-heeled. And not only girls! Stern, cross, very serious grown-up ladies with patent leather hair; pouters, snarlers, gigglers, eye-rollers; funny ones, tragic ones: Cruel Christines, Mean Maries, and Good-time Gertrudes. Some who looked like starlets and some who looked like saints. They stood alone, they stood in twos and threes; they whispered, they called; a few of them said nothing, could not be provoked into speech. These dangled keys.

Moving fast, Kevin wondered why fate had drawn him here of all places. He saw and was drawn to a young woman in a doorway—not one of those obvious girls, not one of those who muttered endearments. A discreet, gentle-looking (dismally prim) soul wearing a gray *tailleur,* of all things. In his private scenario, she looked as though, let's see, as though just until the recent past she had attended good schools. Fallen on hard times, her family had delicately asked her to leave and make her way on her own. Without a proper profession she turned one day, not long ago, it seemed to him, maybe even that day itself, to this. . . .

"Good evening," he heard himself say.

She nodded.

"It's cold," he said, "and you're not wearing a coat." His tone was sympathetic, his manner trustworthy. True, he felt a tremble in his groin.

"No, I am not wearing a coat." Tonelessly stated.

"Do you have a coat?" He thought, Am I about to remove my coat and offer it to her? But she was so fragile looking.

"Are you a coat salesman?" She looked him up and down.

"That isn't why . . ."

"It's three hundred francs," she said, looking at his trousers and then on down the street. Toward the Seine. Toward the South of France. Toward Monte Carlo. "A half hour. Four hundred if you're slow."

"I see," said Kevin, in the voice he used when a student had not fulfilled his promise. "I have misjudged . . ." He left it at that, turning angrily on his heel, his misjudgment dying on his lips. New angers whirled in his head. What was I hoping for, dumb son of a bitch? I am not looking for anything, he thought, thought it with all his might. But even so, all this street's to-ing and fro-ing, upping and downing, inning and outing, was having an accumulating erotic effect on him. Maybe, yes, a night of love. But this wasn't the place for LOVE. He imagined the word typed out on his Minitel.

Picking up speed he passed the small, mean Arab and Turkish cafés, the fluorescent-lit sex shops and video stores merchandising sex with the newest borrowed and altered salesword to excite the French—*hard: hard* shows, *hard* couples, *hard* lesbiennes, *hard action*. "Hard times ahead!" he said aloud in a moment of pure abandon. An American hippie, a leftover from another time, hearing him, answered, "Right on, man. How's about some spare change for a cup of coffee and a piece of pie?"

"Right on," copied Kevin, jangling his pockets. He came up with two francs and seventy centimes, which the hippie accepted unpleasantly, shouting after him, "I said a cup of coffee *and* a piece of pie. Cheap bastard."

Adding yet another rejection to the evening.

But soon he found that he'd left the whole mess behind. Except for a few laggards, a few men urinating against walls, and a clutch of transvestites desperately checking their makeup under a broken Pepsi-Cola sign, it was quiet. The big-band parade of the rue St. Denis must have been still blasting away back there but he was out of it, becalmed, and only its reverberations remained in his head. At the river he was stopped dead, because of the margin it provided. Because of the beauty of it.

The illuminations on all the monuments had been turned off and the only lights now were the lanterns, spaced like sentinels along the quays. There was no moon, but in the lamplight the façade bordering the Ile de la Cité had been turned, through some magician's trick, into a stage setting for a provincial town; the family of houses slanted toward each other as though huddling close, all dark, their wavering outlines reflected in the river. I have come here for these moments, thought Kevin, as a barge drifted soundlessly up the Seine. Because there is no place like it in the world and it can never happen again.

Then he was in a taxi; then he was at his front door; then he was up his stairs and back in his apartment. It was two o'clock in the morning.

On a roll, as they said in New York and Los Angeles. The idea of sleep had vanished. Instead, he flung his coat on a chair and found himself switching on the Minitel. YOUR PSEUDO? it blinked, YOUR PSEUDO? He thought, What to call myself? What emblem, carried by a phantom herald across the screens of France to an unseen public, would make him irresistible? Kevin did not hesitate. Typing rapidly he filled in the space between the parted lips: L'HOMME INVISIBLE. He stared at it, fascinated. For a brief second the words stared back, then vanished as the mechanisms whirred into action; a computerized page turned, and an instant later a list of players spread across the screen in front of him.

RIQUIQUI	JEUNE MALHEUREUSE
H CARESS F TEL	H CH NUIT D'AMOUR
F 44A BCBG	QUERIDO, DONDE STAS?
BITTE EN AIR	DEBANDES-MOI
JF CHERCHE UN BEAU MEC POUR L'AMOUR	FARFELUE
PETITE JF CHERCHE MEC SERIEUX	H 40 A-M LIBRE
CLITORDENE	PARISIEN 35A
2 BAD BOYS	MARTHA 37 ANS
H SODOMISE F	SEX STAR
H CH BEAUX SEINS	PUCEAU
TRESORS DE TENDRESSE	CH LIAISON SERIEUSE
HELLO OUT THERE	f pour f
FOXTROT A DEUX (HF)	CAROLINE
MEC A MEC	JF CH CONVERS
VOL DE NUIT	H FAROUCHE
L'HOMME INVISIBLE	JF EXHIBE
ELLE ET LUI CH F	IERE FOIS
CANAILLOU	BAS NOIR

This was but the first page. Kevin read through it in such a dizzied state that nothing properly registered. But as his translating instincts went immediately into action, this is how he saw the screen:

PINTSIZED	UNHAPPY YOUNG LADY
MAN CARESSES FEMALE BY PHONE	MAN WNTS NIGHT OF LOVE
WOMAN 44, WELL BRED	DARLING, WHERE ARE YOU?

COCK IN THE AIR	DEFUSE MY ERECTION
YNG WMAN WANTS HNDSME GUY FOR LOVE	WHIMSICAL
LITTLE LADY WANTS SERIOUS GUY	MAN 40 AFTERNOONS FREE
CLITORIS SPECIALIST	PARISIAN, 35 YEARS OLD
2 BAD BOYS	MARTHA, 37
MAN SODOMIZES WOMAN	SEX STAR
MAN LOOKING FOR BEAUTIFUL BREASTS	VIRGIN (MALE)
TREASURES OF TENDERNESS	SEEKS SERIOUS LIAISON
HELLO OUT THERE	lady for lady
FOXTROT FOR TWO (MF)	CAROLINE
GUY TO GUY	YOUNG LADY WANTS TALK
NIGHT FLIGHT	UNTAMED MALE
THE INVISIBLE MAN	YNG FEML EXHIBITS HRSLF
SHE AND HE ARE LOOKING FOR LADY	FIRST TIME
NAUGHTY BOY	BLACK STOCKINGS

The question trembled. YOUR CHOICE? it asked. YOUR CHOICE? The wonder of it all was that he asked only this of himself: which one? *Which one?* He did not ask why he was there. He had pulled up a chair to the gaming table; the cards, so to speak, had been dealt, and, like any of the other players (though probably newer to the game than the rest of them) he was living in the absolute present, accompanied by the bewitching win-or-lose nervousness that unites all gamblers and synthesizes the human condition.

Because it had a nice sound, all those T's, E's, R's, and s's promising warm comfort on a cold shore, he chose TRESORS DE TENDRESSE. "I am a thirty-six-year-old American living in Paris," he wrote. "I am a sculptor, a translator, a radio announcer, and an English teacher. I . . ."

He sat back. I what? I . . . I need? But no: needfulness was best kept under wraps. Like poverty, joblessness, illness, disfigurement, *need* was ill-favored with demagnetizing elements. Need is is the element that everyone flees from.

"I would like to know who you are," he added, pressing a button to send the message. His words were electronically ripped away from his view. Now they were winging their way through the night.

MESSAGE SENT, it said. The blank screen was immediately replaced by the list of participants. YOUR CHOICE? it asked, asked, asked again, blinking steadily. This Minitel was as greedy as a casino. Kevin hungrily reread the list. The JF EXHIBE certainly was an alluring prospect. Surely she must already be in deep communication with the TWO BAD BOYS. Still, why not try? He began to write what he thought might be a witty message when all at once at the top of the screen MESSAGE WAITING blinked seductively. It was a thrilling moment, suddenly reminding him of some time in the dim past when in his school days he'd received an anonymous Valentine card. He quickly pushed the appropriate buttons, and there in the darkness of his room, the print on the screen displayed MESSAGE from TRESORS DE TENDRESSE to L'HOMME INVISIBLE.

> In answer to your message, I am searching for a very good-looking young man with a lithe body and not much brain, as I have but one night a month to myself. You, Invisible Man, do not sound like that young man to me.

Jolted, Kevin sat back in his chair trying to absorb what had just happened. This machine was not a funny gadget, a second cousin to those video games. There genuinely existed somewhere out there a real person, a woman calling herself Treasures of Tenderness, who had the power to hurt or to please. She had read Kevin's message and was responding to it. Her return message was transferred, by an electronic system whose workings were beyond his comprehension, into his living room. He reviewed this information several times, trying, as though learning a set of rules, to get it straight. A real person, out there. Just as he was real to her.

"You call yourself Treasures of Tenderness," he wrote back with genuine feeling, still stung, his fingers punching the keyboard, "and it turns out that you're simply looking for a hot time." He then corrected this last part to read "a sexual event. I am sorry to say this, but you misrepresent."

The reply was almost immediate. "Do not reprimand me," said Treasures of Tenderness. "I intend to give a great deal of tenderness to the young man who fits the description I've sent to you. Adieu."

Kevin sat very still, listening to the late night sound of the occasional traffic beneath his window. This was not leading to the fun and games that Sasha Wittenburg had indicated. Further rejections were not what he needed. Much sobered, he stared at the Minitel. Other messages awaited. Though his heart might have been mildly wounded, his fingers were poised, ready to reply.

HELLO OUT THERE: I cannot imagine anyone with a shred of self-confidence calling himself an invisible man. However, I'm interested in learning why. It is a refreshing change. Tell me more about yourself. Maybe you're into analysis? I hope you are a nonsmoker. I am an American.

"Oh, God!" he said aloud. "She sounds like someone I went to school with."

"I don't think we're very suited to each other," he wrote back, "but do not be discouraged. The list of possibilities on your screen is long. The night is young."

VOL DE NUIT: Welcome to our group. I have not seen your name here before. Send me further details when you have the time.

MEC A MEC: Since you're invisible anyway, this is what I'd like you to be. Between 26 and 29. Six feet tall with a swimmer's body. Intelligent, healthy, amusing, and great in bed. Please let me know whether you are intending to reveal yourself in this particular form, and if you are, whether you could get yourself right over to my apartment on the Place des Vosges before morning.

Kevin found himself smiling. "If I were all those things," he wrote, "I wouldn't be sitting here at two-thirty in the morning fiddling with a machine."

JEUNE MALHEUREUSE: I am, quite honestly, many people's idea of a beautiful woman, with long blond hair and patrician features, though I have a rather melancholy smile. I tell you this because I live cloistered in a small chateau near the Puy de Dôme attending to my parents, both of whom are ill. Tonight I could not sleep. Outside it is snowing, and I feel that if I don't make some human connectio

The message broke off.

Kevin turned away and stared out of the window into the night sky. A mauve haze obscured the stars. He pictured her, pictured it all: the small chateau in the dour Auvergne, the snow lightly falling outside her shuttered windows . . . He tried to imagine himself getting on a train, meeting her on the station platform. When in a frenzy he began to reply to her, the Minitel interrupted him, indicating in the upper left-hand corner that JEUNE MALHEUREUSE had broken off. ELLE EST PARTIE, it said.

What had happened, oh Jeune Malheureuse! Had one of her sick parents knocked with a cane on the ceiling above her head, summoning her to come at once? Who was there to rescue her as the snow swirled past the stones of her small chateau, coating the paths and the long drive lined with cypresses? These questions existed on a level just underneath his consciousness, so that merely the palest edges of them were revealed to him. His concentration was fixed instead on something larger than that romantic chateau scenario, though the substance of it kept evading him. Had he looked carefully he might have seen that this thing, this gadget, this unholy machine, the Minitel, was precisely what he had been waiting for. But he did not want to look. He knew only that he was becoming more and more disturbed by all this, that the machine was equipped with the ability to hurt, amuse, irritate him, make him anxious, unsettle his life. Another MESSAGE WAITING lit up the screen. He was about to avoid it, to switch off the Minitel, but he left it on. Following the unexpected turmoil of the day, maybe the long night still held something in its own unfathomable machinery. He pushed the button one more time.

4

. . . .

He was in a taxi, propelled forward by circumstances at this ungodly hour, trying not to think about the ticking meter (more expensive after midnight), trying not to imagine the ghastly shape he'd be in by the time morning came (two hours away), for Kevin was one of those people who fear breaking down completely if they do not have eight hours of uninter-rupted sleep. Now, heading toward the rue Bois le Vent, he was beset by worries, a lavish entertainment he allowed himself more frequently than might have been provident, given that one day he might use up his supply—when he really might need it, that is—of worry. Throughout his thirty-six years, Kevin had frequently been told that he worried too much. Maybe he simply exhibited his worrying more than others did. But he figured privately that the worry quotient of most people was about the same. This theory connected to his even more interesting view that in summing up a life—any life—everyone would turn out to have been born with the same potential for pleasure and pain, happiness and despair, the ratio, no matter how it might outwardly appear, as reliable as a heartbeat. Possibly it would be evident in a simple equation yet to be discovered, an essential, shattering code that was evading scientists and philosophers and had remained uncracked. The idea that it all balanced out equally for everyone often sustained him during his bad moments.

And this was one of his bad moments, for in addition to his worries about the amount of sleep he was missing and the cost of the taxi ride, he began to seriously worry about what he had gotten himself into. Maybe the girl waiting for him would turn out to be some kind of a nut case. Or a mugger luring victims to the rue Bois le Vent in order to rob them and steal their passports or their *cartes de séjour.* Until this moment he had been flooded by erotic anticipation. PETITE JF CHERCHE MEC SERIEUX had written him a message that said something like this: Wasn't the winter awful, the nights so long, and Paris, didn't he agree? was a cold city without heart.

Oh, yes, he agreed. There he was, and there she was, and so he'd written back, encouraged, saying, flat out, without a preamble: Given how cold and heartless it was out there, two souls alone on a winter night, *shall we meet? I mean now?*

Meet? At this hour? Without first having . . .

Yes, he'd written. It had been a long evening. He had no more heart for anything long-winded. *Yes, now.*

But, you know, I'm not the kind of girl who just . . .

Of course not. And I'm not the kind of guy who expects . . . But we've got to start somewhere.

Well, if it's understood that . . . And you don't try to . . . Well, yes, why not? *Why not now,* she relented. You sound like a nice person.

And gave him her telephone number.

In the post-midnight madness of the moment, they then exchanged, verbally, only a few relevant details. Her accent, from the Midi, was, well, *of the people.* Though earnest.

He'd forgotten to mention much about himself and she forgot to ask. But she revealed that she was *petite,* with dark hair, and young.

And what do you do? Kevin thought to ask.

Je suis une domestique.

Ah, yes, he'd said, a maid. Well, ah . . .

In a large household, she added, the family being out of town for the week.

Now in the taxi Kevin recalled her saying, and rather petulantly, too, I have had my share of hopes and dreams, just like everyone else.

A maid, he couldn't resist thinking. Of course. She even talks like a maid. A disgusting, priggish reaction which he compensated for immediately by having sounded even more eager than he felt. He quickly got her address and now he was on his way.

The driver, an extremely elegant gentleman whose career intentions in their time must have undergone alarming changes, swung down the rue du Bac, turned toward the quai d'Orsay and pressed on toward Trocadéro. When he reached the immense steel girders supporting the unilluminated Eiffel Tower he stopped to consult his map.

"It's the rue Bois le Vent that I want," said Kevin urgently.

"I heard you the first time," snapped the driver. "I am not unfamiliar with it. The rue Bois le Vent is situated next to the Musée des Lunettes et Lorgnettes de Jadis, just past the Métro Muette."

Kevin shifted in his seat, offering up, despite himself, a small laugh. It was an outlandish thought, his lust-driven mission just down the street from a museum dedicated (so French) to eyeglasses and lorgnettes. But his observations were interrupted by the driver, who was not through: "I'm looking at the map to find the street *direction.* Not to find the street. Unlike most of the boulevards in Paris the streets, as you might know, are one-way. And I won't be hurried.''

"Excuse me,'' said Kevin, irritated at having lost the thread of his own thought. "I beg your pardon. You must forgive me.'' This bit of overly polite irony was lost on the driver who, now that he'd discovered the information he was seeking, replaced his steel-rimmed eyeglasses in their zippered case and zoomed across the Pont d'Iéna, circling the Trocadéro where a small but sturdy frieze of young men slouched and posed and made vaguely seductive gestures that seemed to be of agreeable interest to the drivers of the large cars cruising slowly along the road, as a certain number of them were pulling over to the curb.

Even at four in the morning, this town has but one thing on its mind, Kevin thought. And I am part of it. The sheer idiocy of this adventure began to excite him, connecting him to the human race and its shared ratio of pleasures and pains. Ever since her Midi-accented self-description, he had been imagining a voluptuous pink maiden, with dark, dark eyes, heavy eyebrows, and red-cherry lips; maybe even a birthmark placed just *there* on her cheek. A Spanish melon-maid, soft inside, *petite,* as she said, not yet fully ripe . . .

"We are here. In time, I would think,'' said the driver as though having read his heated thoughts.

When Kevin got out of the car (did he feel his joints creak?) he noticed a pale figure in the shadows behind the wrought iron gate. What he saw was such a tiny thing that he perceived it as an imaginary night-sprite caught midstep, hopping from leaf to leaf.

"Is that you?'' he whispered.

With a hand covering its—or rather, her—mouth, tittering, she vigorously nodded her head. Then she beckoned him in, staying there in the shadows until the gate closed behind him.

Kevin blurted out, "God, you're so . . . you're such a child!"

"And you!" she said. "I didn't think you would be so *old!*" She led him in through the servants' entrance, past the huge, gleaming kitchen and the small, dimly lit pantry, to a servant's room uniquely cramped. Motioning him over to a straight-backed walnut chair, she arranged herself on the cot, where she took up no more room than a curled-up poodle.

Kevin stared at her, looked around the room and then down at his shoes, which in fact were pinching at the heel, the same moccasins he had worn to dinner with Sasha. So long ago. When he was still young. He'd meant to change them.

She said, "I'm like I told you, no?"

"Yes," he said, looking over. "You have dark hair and you're young. And, ah, small."

Such an opalescent waif was she that he suspected, seating himself in the shade cast by the low-watt lamp, that she might not yet have finished growing. Flannel underclothing peeped out from under her little peasant blouse. Her black hair was short, and her little feet were tucked under her, revealing a pair of doll-like patent leather pumps. Perturbed, tired, starved for something he could not possibly have found here, Kevin sighed, and the world's woes were contained in it. Then, rather biblically, he nodded his head. "I guess I didn't expect . . ."

There was a pause. They looked at, and then away from, each other. Was she as surprised as he? What had she expected to emerge from the taxi when it drew up? A dream prince, surely. This thought brought a rush of charity toward her. "Look, you're such a kid. Maybe you can tell me what you were hoping to find, playing with the Minitel."

"I want to find a boyfriend."

"But—"

"And as I say, you are too old. But on the phone—"

"On the phone I was younger, yes?"

She nodded her head and tried to smile.

"So, here we are," he said, looking at her legs curled under her, noting the near absence of breasts and then her tiny, pale face, its strong Gallic features waiting for the years to catch up. Now he felt an unaccountable sexual stirring that surprised him, for this elf perched on a cot was certainly not a creature who'd inhabited any of his dreams. Still, none of us is perfect.

"You ought to find a boyfriend quite easily," he said, just to keep talking.

She shrugged. "Well, it's not so easy. I'm not as young as *that*. I'm just small. I want to find a boyfriend who, you know, likes a little sort of lady."

He pictured someone crossing the small room in one step to scoop her up, carrying her away to his lair to nuzzle her, lick her, feed on her so that there would be nothing left at all. Like a game bird, a quail, leaving behind only a pathetic little mound of bones.

"Would you like a glass of wine?" she offered.

He said no, thanked her, and referred to the lateness of the hour.

"Well, you seem to be a nice, sensitive man. I can tell."

"Ah . . . yes," he said. "That's me, all right." Having decided by then to release himself from any libidinal responsibilities, Kevin became paternal: "Listen, it's true, I am a nice man. You've got to be careful. You play that Minitel and you might get a not-nice man." He found himself stuttering. His concentration had gone. He was now at the door.

"And you?" she said, standing up to her almost five feet. "You be careful too. I could be a crazy girl, call the cops,

say that you came in through the window. But I wouldn't.''
She hesitated. ''I wonder . . .'' she began in another voice,
appraising him anew.

''What?'' he asked, though he did not care what she wondered.

''Well, I have an aunt around your age. She's a widow.
Maybe you'd—''

''I really have to be going,'' he said. He turned back as
he got outside. ''I hope you don't mind my asking, but is
this your first time on the Minitel?''

''Yes!'' she said, giggling.

''Well, mine too,'' he admitted.

''Do you think,'' she said, ''that all the rest of them are
misfits, too?''

But he pretended not to hear and, yawning nervously, he
walked to the nearby taxi stand and waited. And waited.

Great, he thought. Fix me up with Auntie. Just what I
want. A widow, too. I play with the Minitel and find myself
a dwarf who also happens to be a maid. A maid who has the
audacity, as soon as I walk in the door, to say that I'm too
old! Meanwhile Treasures of Tenderness is sprawled on a
moonlit bed, covered by a sleeping judo jock, and Young
Female Exhibits Herself has picked up all the towels and is
now safely sleeping after several sold-out performances. And
look at me! (And here, instead, he looked out of the taxi's
window at the dark, mysterious streets where not a light shone
in a window, and the traffic lights, now neither red nor green,
blinked a neutral amber, all restraints suspended till day-
break): the Invisible Man gliding through a veiled and silent
Paris with nothing to show for it except a vision of other
people's adventures and thirty bucks worth of taxi fares.

Alone. A fine finish for the night. Sasha Wittenburg would be proud of me.

And then, how amazing! Home again on the rue St. Placide, overcome by the confluence of the night's images, in some mindless orgiastic seizure he flipped the switch once again on the Minitel, now beyond himself, now with barely enough imaginative energy to type as a pseudo an X in the offered space. Was his crazed aim to discover whether at five o'clock in the morning anyone was still out there, on the list, in the dead of night? Or had he turned on the machine simply because, after the long, long night, he did not want to find himself totally alone? Or was he still (for the love of God!) looking for an adventure? Fatigue protected him from searching for the answer, fatigue and the rapidity with which the machine responded. When the list spread itself before him, he was overwhelmed to see that not only were there about forty people still at it, but that one of them was calling himself VISITING STUD.

Awakened, astonished; for a moment it put a fire under him.

"Oh boy, oh boy, oh boy," he muttered aloud, filled with the thrill of wickedness. "Hi, stranger!" he wrote, typing like someone deranged. "New in town?"

Sending it off in a flash, Kevin leaned forward as though to consume the screen, knowing he would not have long to wait.

VISITING STUD instantly replied. "Sure am. Does your X mean X-rated?"

"Oh," X enthused, answering him as quickly, "just a silly pseudo. I have no imagination, I suppose. And you?" In his head his own voice piped up like something from the sound track of *Some Like It Hot*.

VISITING STUD answered: "Staying in a four-star hotel in

gay Paree. Evening long. Discos dreary. Couldn't sleep. King-size bed. Am H'wood producer looking for starlet material. Want to try your luck?''

"Oh, boy, oh, boy. A Hollywood producer."

"Right you are. So tell me about yourself."

The sheer outrageousness of it! Tapping into a private fantasy, like X-raying a mind. The opportunity to trick Sasha Wittenburg flickered as beguilingly as the cursor waiting for his response. YOUR MESSAGE? it asked greedily. YOUR MESSAGE? God damn it! He got you into this. Make a date with him. Offer him the time of his life. Or tell him who you really are. He'd be thrilled for you! YOUR MESSAGE? But Kevin Korlov was, as the tiny waif had said, a nice man. He could go no further with the game. He sat there staring at the screen as Sasha Wittenburg's message stared back at him. A middle-aged Middle European art dealer, who seemed, until this evening, to have elegantly assembled all the pieces of life's puzzle. Trying to get through the desperation of the long winter night hours by inventing another self.

Kevin stood up, glaring at Sasha, at all of them sending and receiving their miserable, fraudulent messages. Where had he read that imagination was ''that inward eye which is the bliss of solitude''?

Abruptly he switched off the machine, seized by exhaustion, stomach cramps, a foul taste in his mouth, an all-encompassing misery of spirit. Then he fell across the bed like a mock soldier shot in a mock battle. He had removed only his coat and his scarf. Now in slow motion he took off his glasses, put them on the night table, pinched the bridge of his nose, then closed his eyes and tried to fall asleep. In a final effort to save himself, to avoid the whole evening's great onrushing wave, he managed to duck under all that had happened, clutching vainly at his small concerns.

Whether his lecture on adverbs would go without a hitch. Whether the loafers he'd been wearing needed to be widened by a shoemaker. And whether he might make another attempt the following evening at preparing the veal casserole. Reminding himself, just before sleep finally overtook him, to buy the onions.

5

. . . . . .

Everything wobbled and blurred. Kevin stood unsteadily in front of his class and tried to keep a cool head, ducking under the mudslide of memories from the night before. The problem, among others, was to teach his students, in addition to *besides, nonetheless,* and *however,* the differences between *nevertheless, still, yet, moreover,* and *incidentally.* Although it was February and the place was poorly heated it occurred to Kevin that he might have a fever; the classroom seemed tropically warm, and he felt, standing there, that his feet were sinking, mired in some ooze flooring the swamp of faces before him. But he managed to get through it somehow, leaving his puzzled pupils to thrash out on their own the incompletely explained nuances of these and other similar words. He assured the class that all this might come in handy one day. Usually so firmly in control, Mr. Korlov lurched homeward.

At the corner of St. Germain des Prés near Le Drugstore a beat-up black Citroën, driven recklessly, narrowly missed him, its bumper dragging, sending up angry sparks. Was it an omen? Jittery anyway, his hangover combining with the emotional, gastronomic, erotic, and scenic pileup of last evening's experiences, Kevin stood for a full minute against the wall in front of the Monoprix, discreetly assuming that slightly rocking yoga stance. The shock of this near accident greatly disturbed him, for he had long ago developed a fear of Death by Car. Two women on an obvious shopping spree stopped to ask him whether he was feeling well, their apricot poodle eyeing him suspiciously. With a forced smile he answered that he was quite well, thank you, wondering whether he would make it all the way home without some nasty, public incident. Everyone zooming past him seemed bent on errands or appointments; everyone seemed to be in fine health, full of vitality and laughter and easy friendships. And young. He began to feel once again like the outsider he always suspected he might be, an indication of how vulnerable he was this afternoon. There was no denying that he was all shakes and shambles. He did not stop at the supermarket, forgoing the promised onions and an encounter with the check-out girl. Finally he achieved the rue St. Placide and dragged himself cautiously up the four flights of heavily waxed and exceedingly slippery wooden stairs. Everything, it seemed, was fraught with danger; his entire life was rickety at its foundations. He was grateful not to bump into Mrs. Bomwalla for another round of aphorisms or epigrams, or whatever they were.

It felt to him like midnight, yet it was then only five in the afternoon. He climbed back into bed and the hours ahead presented themselves as long and as flat as a road across the Sahara. He discovered that he couldn't sleep, that he was both fatigued and restless, listening to the early evening sounds coming through the windows and walls, the high-low sirens of the police cars (had another bomb gone off?), and the honking of horns that always coincided with a sudden rainfall. Periodically an auto alarm would pierce the air, the French having enthusiastically adopted this recent import that coincided so nicely with their territorial preoccupations. It was already pitch dark. Soon the cooking odors from the apartment across the hall would insinuate themselves through his front door; then, from upstairs, the spectacled child there would begin to practice her simplified Chopin Etudes, making the same mistakes as yesterday and the day before, and he would oblige himself to correct them, like it or not, humming the right notes loudly over her wrong ones. Then the clatter of dishes, the muted babble of dinner conversation coming through the walls; then the neighboring television sets would blare in unison. It was only on weekend nights and quite late that the bedsprings just above his ceiling would creak rhythmically and—who knows?—passionately, and a moan might escape into the air over his head. It entered his mind that aside from the soap opera's phony upper-class dialogue having been dubbed into French, he might just as well have been living in South Bend, Indiana. What was happening, he wondered, to the illusion of Paris that just yesterday had still been so thrilling to him?

Something was wrong, out of kilter. It wasn't that he'd grown too used to those periodic two-night visits from the Piano Teacher, it wasn't that he didn't have friendships or cultural interests or the natural curiosity that keeps a person young and reasonably involved. It was just that—he had to face it—his life had no resonance. Well, the dog had to be walked, he would take him as far as the Seine. On clear evenings, standing on the Pont Royal, the monuments could all be seen, illuminated, proclaiming the glory of the republic. It never failed to reinforce his decision to live in such a place as Paris. "Come on, General," he said, holding the leash high. As though in harmony with Kevin's effort to pull himself free, the dog tried to fly into the air, boosting its body upward on tiny legs. ''Time for you to see the spectacle,'' he added. Time for me, too, he thought.

They meandered through the streets, along the shadowy quays, across the lantern-lit bridge and back again, stepping into the warmth of a corner café on the rue du Bac where the strange tall-and-short of them was greeted by indulgent smiles of good will. Invigorated by all this and by the crisp air, Kevin headed home. The domestic scene that awaited (he had forgotten to turn off the lights) ought to have pleased him: the lamplight falling just so across the book on the table, the comfortable chair adjacent: inviting the youngish man in Paris to have a bookish evening at home. But Kevin briskly crossed the room and turned on the Minitel.

He clenched his jaw with anticipation. The vein in his forehead throbbed. GILDA, he typed with determination. Prepared, this time, to get it right.

The lips appeared. He inserted L'HOMME INVISIBLE into the blank space, the screen went blank, and it was followed in a lightning flash by this:

JEUNE MALHEUREUX	MINITEL ROSE
ALLUMEUSE	AMOUREUSE
TRIANGLE CH QUAD	DU BEAU LINGE
FEMME CALINE	PAS MOCHE *DU TOUT*
BOMAL	GIGOLO CH GIGOLETTE
FEU FOLLET	FEMMES JE VOUS AIME
L'HOMME INVISIBLE	FEMME SOUS SOIE
CH EXHIBE SUR FENETRE	TURKISH BOY LOOKS 4 LOVE
H MARIE TRAVESTI CH IDEM	DOMINITAS
M NAGEUR CH PLONGEUSE	RIEN QUE CALINS

F CH DIAL F OU H	23 CMS
VOL DE NUIT	VOYAGE EXOTIQUE

and so on. Which Kevin rapidly translated as:

UNHAPPY YOUNG MAN	MINITEL ROSE
FLIRT	AMOROUS LADY
TRIANGLE LOOKS FOR	SNAPPY DRESSER
QUADRANGLE	
AFFECTIONATE LADY	NOT BAD LOOKING *AT ALL*
GOODLOOKING MALE	GIGOLO WANTS GIGOLETTE
WILL OF THE WISP	LADIES I LOVE YOU
THE INVISIBLE MAN	WOMAN UNDER SILK
WNTS TO WTCH EXHBIST	TURKISH BOY LOOKS 4
AT WINDOW	LOVE
MARRIED TRANSVSTITE	DOMINATRIX
SEEKS SAME	
M SWIMMER SEEKS F DIVER	NOTHING BUT CUDDLING
F WNTS DIALOG WTH	9 INCHES
F OR M	
NIGHT FLIGHT	EXOTIC TRIP

Lights flickered. YOUR CHOICE? YOUR CHOICE? The screen was alive with light. Paris, the city of light! Who could have imagined this city-within-a-city, pulsing with a life of its own! He felt a thrill pass through him as the roll call unfolded, a thrill that lifted him away from his isolation and into the realm where all the Others dwelled, similar souls sitting at their Minitels awaiting contact with each other. Forget everything that he'd felt the night before. He had been overtired, unable to see the beauty of it. It was a glorious list of the liberated, each of them exploding with their own tale to tell, vivid and unrestrained before him, in no way like those Personals columns in the magazines and newspapers where so-called singles inserted ads with box numbers and sat back waiting for the mail to arrive, as it might, a week later, perhaps the following month, at a moment altogether disconnected to the hour they spent laboring over the precise wording of the advertisement. This Machine was immediate. Now. In a sudden, shattering moment the screen presented to the viewer its players (in whistle-stop towns across the plains of Picardy, along the ragged Norman coastline bordering the Atlantic, high in the mountains of the Auvergne), each of them, for whatever reasons that drew them there, in front of their screens; each of them living in the precise present. And instantly accessible. Or so it seemed.

As if welcoming him to the club, VOL DE NUIT immediately sent a message. "Welcome once again. Thought you'd left us," it said. "I would still like to know more about you."

And then, before he had a chance to thoroughly absorb the list or to answer the message—still dazzled by what he was looking at—another message came through.

It was from FEMME SOUS SOIE. On the screen it seemed to shimmer with a particularly unearthly light. "I am asking your forgiveness," it said.

His forgiveness!

"My forgiveness?" he wrote back in haste, ignoring all else. "But what have you done?"

"I have done you a disservice and I have suffered for it. You see, last night I gave myself another name. And after sending you a message, I felt . . . that perhaps I was not being fair to you. I had chosen the name TRESORS DE TEN-DRESSE. But, you see, I had so many messages to answer, long ones, extremely detailed, some of them quite passionate, some of them—if I may put it that way—arousing. Others were crude and still others made no sense. No clarity. Of course, that is to be expected. This, you understand, is a communication based on contradictions, on darkness and light.''

''On fantasies, do you mean?'' he wrote.

Her return message was more sober. ''The people you see on these long lists are most frequently sitting in the darkness of their rooms. This allows them to write things and refer to themselves in ways they might never imagine revealing in what one might call the real world. And last night, after I managed to clear my mind of all those messages I received and replied to, I finally thought of sending word to you. I had continued to regret what I'd said. But you were no longer there.''

Kevin allowed himself to answer, ''I'd found someone else more sympathetic.''

''I am not surprised,'' she wrote. ''I note that you are foreign, even though I see now that your French is remarkable. There is always something, you know, a shade of meaning unclear, a nuance. I noted that with your first message. But, of course you understand that foreignness in Paris is essential for a romantic encounter. The French, particularly the Parisians, adore accents and a somewhat faulty use of their language. I think it makes them feel superior, which is their natural inclination.''

''And you? Do I detect a foreignness in your voice?— though how can I use the word *voice* when I haven't yet heard you speak? This is such an extraordinary way to meet, without a specific image, only a fantasy to follow.'' Kevin had now rashly borrowed her somewhat florid style for himself. ''And then, of course, later, if we manage to speak on the phone, comes the voice, and then the actual face, the person. There are so many hurdles ahead.''

"You write poetically, so poetically. In fact, I cannot imagine you as anything else. A poet, an artist of some kind. When you wrote last night that you teach English I feel as though you are disguising your true profession, your true nature! But no matter, no matter, at least for now. I will accept what you say. Yes, to answer your question, I am not what you might call altogether French. I am partly Russian, partly French, partly from the Argentine."

Kevin studied her latest message. It was time, he felt, to make some move toward the real world. "I don't understand the next step," he wrote. "How, where do we begin? I must admit that I am new at this."

"You will telephone me. No, no! I will telephone you. That's it. I will phone you at a given hour, a phone appointment. We cannot begin unless there is some formality."

"I agree with you absolutely. I am sending you my phone number. And I will be at my telephone at exactly what hour?" He was punchy. He was writing with an accent. It made no difference. He added his number.

"At midnight," she wrote. "It will allow us the thrill of waiting." And when he answered back she was no longer there.

The seductive list before him no longer mattered to Kevin. Dazed, he sat before the blank screen, his glasses on the desk, rubbing his eyes. He was aware of his heart beating, of the sound of his breath, of an anticipation that sent vibrations throughout his body. He walked over to his one comfortable chair (bought at the flea market, though reupholstered, and rather expensively, in a Napoleonic pattern of golden bees and laurel wreaths on a burgundy ground) and picked up his book, glancing with a pretended calm at the slow-motion clock, an Art Deco wonder in marble that seemed to want to thrust its fins into the sky. Aware, too aware of the ponderous ticking, he put on his coat and his scarf and went downstairs (without The General) to search for yet another nearby café that might still be open. At the corner of the rue de Rennes he looked to the north, noting the ancient, illuminated church of St. Germain and then to the south, looking up at the illuminated Montparnasse tower, the highest skyscraper in Europe. Kevin said into the night air, "Ah, Paris," inhaling deeply: How variable its history from one street corner to another! How unpredictable its promise from one moment to the next! Even in this grayest night of winter, it dazzles! Blinded by this newly acquired vision he was not concerned about his excessive enthusiasm or how long it might last.

The warm, pale light behind the frosted windows beckoned him inside. He smiled to the proprietor, whose hands were immersed in soapy water. For this he received a polite nod in return, and they struck up an unexpectedly pleasurable conversation about the weather as Kevin Korlov, neighbor on the nearby rue St. Placide, drank his coffee at the bar. He put a coin in the pinball machine and in his zeal caused *tilt* to appear before he finished his game. But no matter, no matter; no omen was intended. He ordered a cognac. Almost immediately his digestive system rebelled, and, now hiccuping, he walked once around the block and returned home. At midnight he was next to the phone. It did not ring. It did not ring at 12:10, nor at 12:20.

"I am sorry that I am late," she said on the phone toward one a.m. "One must never expect idle people to be prompt. They will always find ways to waste time."

"I'm glad you called," he said, masking any desperation. "I am genuinely glad that you called."

"And now that I hear your voice," she said, her own voice a purr, "I, too, am glad. It is beautiful as I'd hoped it would be. I think . . ." she hesitated. "Yes, I think we may have created something extraordinary."

6

. . . .

He sat in the dark, the faded farmhouses and the wooden carts now obscured on the walls by the deepest night shadows. Only a slanting light, so pale that without the surrounding dark it would never have been perceived, pierced through his curtains and stole across the very edge of his headboard, fluctuating there as though mildly suggesting that he put his weary head down against the pillows and stop this madness. But he remained untempted, sitting on the edge of the bed in total darkness, the telephone pressed for dear life against his ear. And, because of the dark, the absolute stillness, and the need within to be heard by another human being, the conversation took on a dimension and importance that exceeded any natural limits. Two strangers in Paris talking to each other in the dead of night: She, imperially seductive in the way she spoke—as though, having granted him her auditory favors, she was not sure at all about the rest, waiting to see how he shaped up, whether he could carry his spiritual, intellectual, and emotional weight, or whatever else she was testing him so charmingly about.

The specific strands of conversation, on later reflection,

would not be remembered. He recalled certain things: that the meaning of solitude was somehow discussed, as was (God help him) Camus, Pascal, and the impact of strikes and demonstrations on what he remembered referring to as the fabric of France. But if his concentration on these specifics was poor it was because all the while this conversational game was going to and fro between them, Kevin kept wondering how he might achieve a meeting with her in the Real World, so hesitant had she seemed at first to consent to it.

In an unguarded moment Kevin said, "Illusions have no real meaning for me. They're lifeless things, like—oh, I don't know. Like shells. If things won't come to life, I would prefer to let them go."

She considered this. "And for me," she finally replied, "this is not at all true. In fact, I often think that it is the reverse. This bizarre situation, for example, is possible only because of our fantasies. Isn't that the point of the whole exercise? Don't you—"

"Exercise!" he interrupted, his voice almost passionate. "Do you see it as only that?"

"I mean, two disembodied voices, with only our imagination to fill in the rest."

"No!" he said with unusual confidence. "Not for me. I'm having this conversation with you only because I expect you to turn real." He paused for emphasis. "And as soon as possible!" he added. The absoluteness of his conviction surprised them both, for until then the conversation had been rather more poetic.

"All right, then," she said, "I think we *should* meet, after all. Maybe a week from today. Yes. A week from today." Did he hear her turn the pages of her appointment book? "Friday, the twenty-fifth of February. At one o'clock, in front of Charvet. You know it, of course. On the Place Vendôme. I think I'll wear my red Chanel suit. It is a beautiful suit and one of my favorites. The embroidery along the edge of the jacket is a plum color; no, actually, it's more like aubergine. Also, I'll be wearing a black woolen coat, belted, like a dressing gown. As I go to the hairdresser there every Friday, I have lunch just around the corner. There's a small, rather good brasserie. They always keep a table for me.''

He remembered Charvet from that time, six years ago, when he'd just arrived in Paris. He recalled the made-to-measure shirts, the ascots, the luxurious silk robes on display in their window, the shop itself set, between two imposing international banks, into the corner of the Place Vendôme. He had been talked by the gallery owner, Dryfuss, into purchasing an incredibly expensive silk tie there (never quite forgiving himself) to wear to his opening at the art gallery. Yes, he remembered Charvet, and the tie . . . What color was it? he wondered, throwing out a frantic, summoning appeal to his shadowed carts and farmhouses. Bordeaux! he remembered triumphantly. Anyway it was spotted that very night by spilled wine. He'd never gone back to Charvet again.

"Charvet. A wonderful idea. Somewhere I have one of their red ties,'' he contributed.

"All right, then,'' she said, with a finality that suggested her rising from a chair. "But you must tell me what you will be wearing! How will I know you?''

"Ah, of course, of course,'' he said, casting another anxious look around the room. "I'll wear, let's see, a Burberry coat. You know, the kind with a plaid lining . . .''

"The Invisible Man in the Burberry coat,'' she said.

Momentarily flustered, he added, "Well, also a blazer, and khaki pants . . . Look, do we have to wait until next week?'' It was a challenge; she could seize it or let it go. Nervously biting his lower lip Kevin looked around himself, worried about the oncoming solitude.

"But waiting is almost the best part!'' she said as he

continued to scan the darkness of his bedroom. "Oh," she added, struck by a thought. "A small detail, if you'll forgive me. But, you see, it's the one thing . . . I hope you won't be insulted by my asking you . . ."

Immediately his guard went up. She would turn out to be a racist. No, she would give him some impossible task to perform, the kind of thing that royalty was always extracting in fairy tales. He would be required to bring her a golden hen.

She seemed to be deliberating.

"Well, you'd better ask me. Ask me now, right away."

"Well, it's this. You're not very, ah, *small*, are you?"

"Small?"

"Yes, I mean your stature. You see, it isn't that I am excessively tall, though I am a bit taller, for a woman, than usual . . ."

"No," he said, exhaling with relief. "No, I'm five ten, five eleven. Just under six feet."

"Oh, that is nice," she said, her voice, too, relieved. "I have a terrible problem about tiny people. I simply don't like them. It's one of the few things that I generalize about. I've found that they bustle so, they're so nervous, so full of contention. I think it's that the blood travels such a relatively short distance in them, from here to there, if you see what I mean. Like Yorkshire terriers. It pumps them up early in the morning and runs them at a faster, more aggressive speed throughout the day and into the evening. They make me feel as though I lumber, and actually I am rather agile, having danced in the ballet. But I cannot bear to have my composure shattered by someone constantly nipping at my heels. That's all I meant."

He laughed out loud. So giddy was he, all at once, that for an instant he almost told her about his last night's experience with a very small person on the rue Bois le Vent. But quickly sobered by the realities, he replied, "No, I am not small. You can relax about that." Then, in a voice even more controlled, he added, "If we're speaking of, well, of physical defects, I guess I ought to tell you that I do wear glasses—"

"But I like glasses," she interrupted. "I also love aquariums. I have been told that there is a specific link between the appreciation of men wearing glasses and of tropical fish inside transparent tanks."

Again he laughed. "And," he continued bravely, "as they say so kindly in French, my forehead has lost some of its trimming."

"Dégarni! Oh, good heavens. I like thinning hair. It allows a man a certain vulnerability that is very reassuring. After a certain age men look so stubborn, so uncompromising, with full, thick heads of hair, as though they refused to part with any of it along the way. It implies a certain absence of generosity to me, and it means that they haven't experienced the suffering that other men, particularly young men who lose their hair at an early age, require of themselves."

"You certainly have a generous nature. And a lot of theories . . ."

"Yes, and one of them is to conclude telephone conversations when they amble too much. And so I will hang up now. We are arranged for Charvet at one, and I shall be wearing a red Chanel suit bordered in aubergine, and on top of that a black coat—"

"—of wool, belted but not buckled."

"Precisely. And you will be in a Burberry. Your pants—"

"Tan . . ."

"Tan pants and a blue blazer. No white scarf? No rolled-up copy of the day's *International Herald Tr—*"

"Le Monde," he corrected.

"Yes. Even better. I see it, though I do not want to see

it too clearly. I would prefer to avoid receiving a precise image. Then you would have to live up to it, or down to it. In any case it would ruin everything.''

If she said goodbye, he had not heard it, for the phone went dead.

She was, she had said, thirty-six, though probably—and excusably—this might not have been altogether true. French-Russian-Argentinian, educated in Switzerland and extravagantly multilingual, a wearer of Chanel suits who has her hair done weekly on or near the Place Vendôme after which she lunches around the corner. Try as he might, Kevin could call up no further facts. Ah, yes, tallish. But beyond that it was hopeless. So little to go on, so few specifics. And yet she remained and reappeared in his mind as clearly as a remembered phrase of music. It was her voice, mainly, and the way she had of phrasing things, even though, because of the excitement he'd felt throughout the call, he had not paid the proper attention to the details. What was it she had said? A word in Italian (a language in which, it seemed, she was also fluent). Yes, *redimensionare*—now he remembered—was her favorite word in Italian, though the reason *redimensionare* was her favorite word eluded him. How could he have forgotten this? Why hadn't he paid more attention?

Her name swept him up in its feathery embrace: Lea. It was magic, a sheer miracle, the two of them sharing this remarkable episode in the middle of the night. So bright was she, so mysterious! And yet, and yet . . . there was a terrible seesawing conflict in his worry-ridden heart. Beyond all this magic and mystery filling him, there was this one inescapable fact:

The circumstance of their meeting.

Poor Kevin Korlov's mind found no repose. The Minitel.

How could an absurd computer device plugged into a telephone have been a party to—no, have created—this encounter? Imagine Proust, or James, or Forster, and those civilized
fin-de-siècle situations they created where two people met so
elegantly by chance, introduced by cousins at a soirée, or
playing as youngsters in the Jardin des Tuileries. She had not
been his nurse while he was convalescing, nor a passenger
on a ship who happened to have a deck chair adjacent to his.
It had come about, instead, via a spurious list of randy ex-
hibitionists, neglected rejects, and visiting firemen (Sasha
Wittenburg loomed for an instant like a jack-in-the-box,
sprung from the upholstered back seat of his hired Mercedes). The facts were these: repelled and yet inspired by
this secret of his urbane friend, he had turned on a machine
producing a computerized list of solitary people needing
some communication, and that after an unsuccessful first try
the machine had, like a Las Vegas one-armed bandit, spilled
out an unexpected bonanza. A jackpot.

He tried to convince himself that maybe none of this seedy
stuff had any truck with *his,* Kevin's, exalted communion,
for he could not accept that the enchanted midnight conversation between strangers had come about because of a me-
chanical device. The image was too crass and unacceptable.
He preferred to think of it this way: like a journey on a train,
two passengers finding themselves by chance in the same
compartment at night. That was the kind of meeting it had
been, and the impulse to maintain a romantic discipline was
so strong (and so foreign to him) that after several days he
was almost successful in imagining that he'd met Lea traveling through the French countryside at night.

Maybe Lea was right. Maybe waiting was the best part.

He was certainly making himself available to daydream-
ing. To allow himself time for this activity he gave his students an hour-long written test, poor things. The image of

their meeting on a train was so agreeable that he had begun to extend the metaphor. Perching on the edge of his desk he thought: Trains, he had always delighted in trains. He had heard that in certain fashionable turn-of-the-century Parisian restaurants, fake train windows had been installed adjacent to the dining tables with scenes painted on a hand-cranked canvas so that the romantic couples dining there could imagine that they were traveling . . .

And here he was interrupted by a student inquiring about a mistake in the exam book.

Kevin adjusted his glasses. They had begun to slide downward.

The student was anxious to point out that the teacher, Mr. Korlov, had misspelled a word. He had written *hoarse,* when it ought to have been *horse,* in the question *Complete the following sentences in the conditional past tense of the verb to speak:* 'He _____ in a hoarse voice.'

"No," said Kevin, "that is what I meant. *H-o-r-s-e* is another, similarly pronounced word. I meant *h-o-a-r-s-e,* as I wrote it. Not horse, which is the animal. I do not mean in the voice of the animal." Flustered to have had his musings interrupted, his own voice, he noted, was sounding peculiar. "Just fill in the verb form. I will explain about hoarse and horse later."

The student, silenced, sat back down, and soon the class was lulled again into its quiet scribbling.

So that week Kevin's private landscape felt as unreal as those primitive restaurant scene-a-ramas. He would look up from the desk in the corner of his living room and see a painted scene of Montparnasse rooftops. He would look up from his jerry-built lectern at the Worldwide Language Center to find the frieze of his students staring mutely back. He would glance away from his dreary script at the radio station and catch the plaster statue of the sound engineer caught in midyawn. Deprived of its habitual reality, none of Kevin's scenery could have been as vivid as the memory of the intimacy of that phone conversation.

Finally, his still fresh, still thick, day-at-a-time desk calendar confirmed to him that the date was indeed Friday, the twenty-fifth of February. Lacking Lea's telephone number he had hoped she would call him again to confirm the date. But this was the kind of small, nagging detail that often obstructed his pleasure, and he was determined to overlook it. He put on the specified clothing, stepped out onto the rue St. Placide at noon, and bought his copy of *Le Monde* at the corner kiosk. Because the weather was beneficent he decided to take his time and dawdle through the Jardin du Luxembourg, which, though slightly out of his way, always gave him such pleasure.

The anarchy of imagination! Swooping down it held him helpless in its unaccustomed grasp. This wavering image of someone named Lea thoroughly ignited him, and he now strolled, in a sense, with her on his arm, noting everything, so voluptuously alert to the day that it was almost painful. Crossing the rue de Fleurus he noticed for the first time a plaque placed next to the doorway of a plain nineteenth-century building indicating that Gertrude Stein had lived here with Alice B. Toklas: ''Throughout her twenty-five years in this house she entertained various literary and artistic luminaries of the period'' (it did not mention that they were thrown out of the building, he recalled, in 1938). He found himself musing on these two ladies, imagining them bent against the cold in their heavy winter coats making their combined way down the street toward the market place: Miss Stein, intense and shrewd, sternly talking, Miss Toklas, all spectacles and mustaches, not listening, trying to remember the ingredients they were seeking for tonight's luminous dinner. And although until then he had never given much thought to these ladies, today he allowed himself the luxury of contemplating them, his intention to belong to everything he saw, and to the Paris surrounding and enriching him; Paris, the one city in the world capable of harboring extreme and celebrated individuals, guaranteeing them (because of its implicit superiority in all things civilized) that their lives could be lived out in privacy or anonymity. Stashed away behind the guileless façades were dethroned sovereigns and unremembered despots, time-honored poets and forgotten cover girls. Such was life in Paris that Kevin could have walked past those two biddies (had they still been alive) without a glance.

By now he was in the Luxembourg gardens, loving Paris, loving the sunshine. The sun had brought everybody out. It was just warm enough to play chess, so the chess players were there, hunched over their boards; the lovers were there, hunched over each other; the babies in carriages were there along with their mothers and nannies, the mothers gossiping with each other while the nannies in the background sat separately, dreaming their Senegalese and Sri Lankan and other deprived nations' dreams. The old men were there, bereted, playing *boules* with such concentration that their cigarettes burned down to the nub, staining their fingers and singeing their mustaches. The old ladies, too, were there, some of them wearing fur tippets, some of them with hats, all of them in somber colors; not a bleached granny in the crowd. Seated on benches they stared, in concentrated clusters, into the depths of their own histories. The dogs, however, were not there, the posted signs indicating that they were unwelcome, but their romp and spirit were transfigured into the reeling, skating, swinging, sailboat-spinning children who seemed to be everywhere at once, a sure sign that Paris would go on forever.

Thus marveling at each separate thing, having dawdled too long and now five minutes late, Kevin arrived at the Place Vendôme and walked briskly toward Charvet. And it was then he made his discovery: Charvet was not there. Charvet was gone, vanished. It was hallucinatory. In its place was a bank. An Italian bank. It was not possible. He was absolutely positive that the Place Vendôme contained in its southeast corner the shop called Charvet. She had said, Charvet. You know it, of course, on the Place Vendôme. The emptiness filled him with dread. He turned, walked toward the center of the square's frame in a panic, and found himself across from a jewelry shop called Chaumet. Chaumet is what she must have said. He was an idiot, simply because he had once bought a silk tie at Charvet, to have assumed without even listening carefully, so besotted was he by her voice, that she was speaking of Charvet. Of course you know Chaumet, she'd said, on the Place Vendôme. No wonder she had made no comment when he'd spoken, his voice swaggering idiotically, of his red tie! With hope, with gratitude, his heart lifted, and he scanned the square in readiness for her arrival from around the corner where the square met the rue de la Paix. *I should love it above all things,* he thought, smiling inwardly, for in reading that dialogue—was it less than ten days ago?—he had imagined himself standing on the Place Vendôme. How curious life was, echoing and mirroring everything, putting order into what seemed so disarrayed. He tried not to look at his watch, tried to discipline himself to study the display windows of Chaumet, where shahbanoo-sized jewelry dominated the small cases, destined for those Saudi and Abu Dhabi girls who had clawed their way painfully out of the oil-rich earth in order to merit these outsized rocks.

But finally it had to be admitted that it was one-thirty. There was no way to avoid it. The clocks at the jewelry establishments around the square—for Kevin made the rounds a few times, checking whether, in fact, Charvet *(you know it, of course)* had found itself another home there—the clocks all pointed their minute hands down, down as far as they could possibly go, touching the 6, reaching down like the hands of women when they adjust the heels of their shoes, as Lea herself might have done had she stopped in midstep, flying down the street toward him.

Well, that was that. You mess around in a pigsty and you get mud all over yourself. No one required him to play the rotten Minitel. Let's face it, Sasha Wittenburg had only suggested it as a lark. That smooth art and antique dealer would have looked at him as though he was stark-raving mad if he'd even mildly suggested a *relationship* arising out of that scurvy list of needful creatures. How could he have done this to himself? He walked, head down, out of the square. It was only at the next corner when in anger at a sports car running the light, he looked up at the traffic signal and saw with dismay that this street leading out of the square—a proper street and no longer part of the square itself—continued to call itself Place Vendôme, apparently such a chic address that it was allowed to spill over, so to speak, into this extra block, gilding the real estate there, too; that the shop at the corner with, in its windows, its glorious silks, its robes, its custom-made shirts, having moved its location at some time during the past six years to the spot where Kevin now stood, desperate, because no woman—no man, even—would have waited there for more than half an hour; that this shop, *of course,* was Charvet, and she was gone.

7

. . . . . .

Imagine this: a thirty-six-year-old American man in a Burberry coat wildly crisscrossing the rue des Capucines peering into each café and brasserie at 1:45 on a Friday at their most smoke-filled, wine-stained, overstuffed, crowded, and rowdy moment of the week. Though the urgency of his quest did not pass completely unnoticed, he himself passed, as expected, invisibly. *Someone* was seen scrutinizing the windows, cupping his hands, one in front of each ear, the better to see inside, though anyone taking note of this shrugged. And went on talking. It was dreadful for Kevin, fathoming still quite lucidly, with each hurried stop, the lunacy of his search. How could a grown person expect to pick out of the crowds a woman he had never set eyes on seated at a table for two (reserved for her each week by the kind though obviously harassed proprietor)? Lost, oh, so lost that he stopped for a moment on a street corner with no idea of where he was, or whether he had already crossed to the other side during the delirium of his search, or even what giant thing inside him was propelling him forward, possessed. But he could not pause long enough to look for logic. He was beyond logic, beyond the careful barriers he had so painstakingly erected throughout these long years of coming to terms with the person he thought he was. But the fact was that he had sensed, in the frightening moment that comes but seldom in a lifetime, that this woman, this creature whose voice alone was known to him, might somehow alter his life (though earlier, in calmer moments, he had expected no shattering, no epiphany, just a modulation into another key). And so it was only when he was halfway down the street, running to and fro on the nearby rue Danielle Casanova, that he stopped short, leaned against a storefront (featuring in its window, of all things, spying and eavesdropping equipment), and gave in, gave up, gave out.

Later, after eating his miserable roast chicken alone in a distant brasserie, after stopping at the Worldwide Language Center to pick up his next semester's teaching schedule, after trudging home as the fast-scudding high clouds obscured the sun and the sky turned rapidly into a steel helmet, sanity had begun to return, self-vilification had diminished, and the good, clean balance of life seemed suspended almost within reach. Though still inaccessible.

Kevin tried not to dwell on the whole disaster any longer. In a fit of lingering punishment, he sat over his ledgers totaling up his year's taxes, letting the night fall as it would. It was early evening. The days, he knew, were getting longer; in several months the city would be allotted its lavish share of those endlessly long spring days that vied with Scandinavia's. But alas, not yet; week after week of those relentless gray days that are Paris's best-kept secret had to be gotten through. Now the wind outside was gaining, the temperature dropped to some icy degree, and Paris beyond the window was imprisoned under glass: a paperweight, with its monuments appropriately placed, waiting to be shaken so that the snow might fly this way and that. A soothing image, he thought.

Naturally he had considered making contact with Lea through the Minitel, his only recourse. But it meant entering that arena of lost souls—which is how he'd come to see it, having withdrawn himself so thoroughly from such an association. Yet how else? He would type in his L'HOMME INVISIBLE and in a flash find himself out there on the screen with the Others. And then? How would he be able to figure out which one she was, if indeed she was there at all, either that moment, or another, or another day altogether, or ever again? So clever were the mechanics of the thing, he reflected (for he knew his Homer and kept it at his bedside) that it could have been a game devised by the gods of ancient Greece. He searched for a page and found it, where the lovely gray-eyed Athena flashes down from Olympian heights to stand in Ithaca transmogrified as a sea captain, ascending several stanzas later to become Athena again.

" '. . . as a bird rustles upward, off and gone,' " he read aloud in his best broadcasting voice, " '. . . changing from god to mortal, from mortal to god.' "

Or from one *pseudo* to another. Carefully he replaced the book on the night table, and drummed his fingers with impatience.

If Lea appeared now, who would know in which guise? Or whether she would bother to make contact with him, deigning to forgive him for having so rudely made her wait (presuming, of course, that she herself had shown up at Charvet). Who knew whether the whole thing hadn't been a gag: Lea in reality a transvestite, or a married woman whose husband got his kicks by listening on the extension, or a well-educated patient dialing on a phone from a funny farm, or an elderly diva playacting her way through the long and painful winter night? Or, or. Who knew anything?

Well, all right: he would make one solid try at it. Abruptly he switched on the machine to scan the pseudos. He typed in GILDA, he presented himself as L'HOMME INVISIBLE, an all-new list of applicants spread across the screen, but nothing on it seemed to fit his feathery image of Lea. He could not resist being moved to reply to AMERTUME, a concept somewhere between regret, bitterness, melancholy, and disillusion that precisely suited his mood, but the answer he received back was from a fifty-eight-year-old gentleman in Tours who had recently, he replied at length, lost both his Belgian Shepherd and his wife. By ''lost,'' it was unclear whether they'd simply been misplaced or whether they'd died.

Kevin switched off the Minitel and sat there, determined to face facts. There was nothing further to do. He had been right, all along, to stick to the smooth, unetched surface of reality, to have avoided the things he could not understand. He was right to have accepted a life uncluttered by emotion, Spartan, unembellished by the kind of fantasies others seemed to have. Pondering this, a self-appraisal that might have required him to retreat even further into himself, he was startled by the telephone. Then it *is* true, he thought, reaching for the instrument with a hand that trembled: accumulated concentration focused on the telephone can transmit itself and cause the awaited call! But no: it was a friend ringing up, suggesting a visit the following day to the flea market. Clearly in a collateral agreement with this determination to dwell in reality, his social life was in for an upswing, for a retired cellist, an appropriately deaf, tough old bird, also came through with an invitation, sounding, the way she bellowed it, as though she were daring him to accompany her and a friend to the Comédie Française. He accepted, of course. He even made a few sociable phone calls himself, though none of the recipients were home. He left messages on their answering machines. Amusing messages, he was of the opinion.

What Kevin hadn't expected was that this sense of loss would so quickly leave him. But he'd had so little to go on with Lea (no shared memories; no touch, no glance, no gesture; only a voice, a manner, an unauthenticated vision) that the inevitable emptiness of having lost her was correspondingly protracted, and by midweek he'd almost managed to forget the whole sad thing. Paris stayed cold, though in two days it would be March. Spring, they said, was in the air, but the only evidence of it was that he heard the workmen in a neighboring building—all of them from the Iberian peninsula or Poland—begin to whistle and sing while they sawed and hammered, as though an animated cartoon of foreign birds had arrived on the scaffoldings, precursors of an eventual warmth which might arrive one day. If everyone managed to live through the intervening period.

It was on the evening that he was rushing to the Comédie Française that the phone rang. Naturally, he thought, it would ring when I am halfway out the door and late. He had forgotten the previous days when all his concentration had gone into pestering her, via the invisible airwaves, to telephone.

"This is Lea," she announced.

"Ah, yes. Lea," he replied, keeping his cool.

"There was no possibility for me to let you know that I couldn't come last week. I'd been called away to London and hadn't brought your telephone number with me. I left in such a hurry. I know it is shameful. I've just got back this afternoon."

He paused a moment, continuing to collect himself. "I understand." He felt peculiar, flushed. Maybe it was because he was standing there in his coat and his heavy scarf, and wearing a hat.

"And so I would like to invite *you* to lunch. Are you free tomorrow, at the same time?"

"At the same corner?"

"Yes, why not? In front of Charvet."

"I must admit, I was confused last time. It isn't on the actual Place Vendôme."

"Well, no, now that you mention it, not on the actual square . . ."

"Of course. And I'll be wearing the same—"

"And so will I. The same suit, you know, red, although maybe a different coat. Perhaps . . ."

He looked quickly at his watch. He would be late. He had planned on taking the bus. He would now have to take a taxi, if a taxi could be found. He would get to the theatre just after the curtain went up and they wouldn't let him take his seat until the intermission. His friends would have waited for him and then given him up and gone in, the ample ex-cellist limping angrily down the aisle. They would have left his ticket at the box office. Or with the ticket taker. Maybe he ought to call a taxi rather than wait in vain at the taxi stand. He despised himself for worrying with such abandon. But such was his nature.

"I've got to rush," he said, clearly unable to give this conversation its due.

"As do I, I suppose," she said. "I have tickets to the theatre. Molière. Yet again. It is as ever present as *Swan Lake.*"

"You? You also have tickets to Molière? But that's in-credible . . ."

"Well, not really, when you think of it. After all, we're in Paris. Although," she added, "there is much less theatre here than in London. Or New York, for that matter . . ."

Her calm was in such bizarre juxtaposition to his agitation that it intensified it. "I—I really must go," he exclaimed.

"Until tomorrow, then," she said. Did he hear her suppress a yawn?

And again she was gone.

There were no taxis. By a miracle he caught the bus and was trundled along by a driver so impeccably uniformed, perched so imperiously high on his seat, that he might have been driving Kevin and the other passengers to a ball at Versailles. Kevin, to his own surprise, was not feeling at all joyful. He'd imagined it otherwise, if she'd ever called him, that is; imagined some rush of passionate feeling. But on the contrary, he did not sit there in a delectable daze. He fiddled with his gloves and worried about the lateness of the hour, noting the scenic wonders that slid past his window with an unusual absence of gratitude. Offering themselves to be admired were the Pont Carrousel, the Seine, the Ile de la Cité moored so perfectly off-center in the river, the majestic façade of the Louvre, and, had he hunched himself down to look way up, the Sacré Coeur on the hills of Montmartre. But he remained untouched by everything. Even during the performance—he'd arrived just in time, once again aware that all his worrying was for naught—his mind was occupied mainly with the plot and subplots of Molière. He had no time for idle thoughts. Besides, the elderly cellist kept nudging him in the ribs to ask, her voice booming like the lower notes of a cathedral organ, what was being said on the stage. Only occasionally did it occur to him that *she* was there. And in those moments, he managed to drown out both his bellowing neighbor and the convolutions of Molière and slip into their place a 35-millimeter black and white fragment of *Camille:* Lea, in the guise of Garbo, looked down at him through her opera glasses and he, as Armand, turned slowly around to catch his first glimpse . . .

During the intermission he suppressed his impatience and shuffled up the aisle with his slow-moving friends. He yearned, of course, to rush out into the monumental lobby. Finally positioning himself on one of the marble balconies he surveyed the audience as it filed out of the theatre and moved in ever-changing patterns throughout the wide staircases and columned corridors. It was impossible for him to carry on a normal conversation with his friends or make the effort to shout his inane comments, for his eyes kept sweeping across the hall. This one, that one, the one over there; any of those tall graceful ladies might have been Lea. It was maddening to imagine that she might have been among them, on the arm of one of the elegant Frenchmen chattering away as they strolled by without a glance of recognition. "I've forgotten to buy cigarettes," he said suddenly, not caring whether any of his friends remembered that he did not smoke, and he broke away, out into the night, gulping the air as though parched, circling the Place de l'Opéra until finally calmed by its animation, the traffic, the crowds. As soon as he had regained his composure he returned to his seat. There, he found his hostess being massively assisted into her seat. "Thought we'd lost you," she snapped. You almost did, he said to himself.

Finally back home, Kevin noted that his answering machine had recorded one call, and after taking off his coat, hanging it up, putting his scarf and gloves carefully in a drawer, he rewound it.

The feathery voice had left the following message: "I

really despise being what you Americans call scatterbrained, a word, by the way, that I love. But in thinking about it, given how cold it is these days, why on earth are we meeting on a street corner? And why are we going to a noisy brasserie? It is quite clear that neither of us has thought this through. Therefore I've made a reservation for one-thirty at a small restaurant I think you will like. Now, I'm not altogether sure I'll be wearing that red suit. I will certainly be wearing a *hat,* a broad-brimmed hat. I almost forgot; the restaurant is on the rue de l'Arbre Sec, on the north side of the rue de Rivoli and very near the Louvre des Antiquaires. It also happens to be the street—'' The beep sounded there, depriving Kevin of the rest of it.

The following morning it rained. A wind had sprung up overnight, the cold had remained, and now there was a mighty squall turning the streets and sidewalks into canals full of hooting cars and splashed pedestrians. The concierge muttered only to herself as she mopped the stairs, the newspaper vendor snatched at his coins; on the Métro Kevin encountered a racist quarrel between four scruffy youths and gave them a wide berth before taking his seat and opening his copy of *Le Monde.* A watery wino accosted him as he emerged from the steps at the Etoile, and by now completely drenched and ill-tempered, he sat down to transmit, by the miracle of broadcasting, his program for the day: ''The Grandeur of France: Fact or Fiction.'' Grandeur indeed. Straying briefly from the text, he permitted himself to say that the French were justifiably considered the world's prime complainers, overly suspicious and underdeodorized. This observation popped out of him as though some other, raging Kevin demanded to be heard. It jolted the sound engineer, who had been drowsing at his reels. Kevin did not bother to apologize. He never really believed there was a listening audience for this thing anyway. When he finished the program he walked wordlessly out of the studio, grabbing his wet umbrella and heading for the Métro without making his customary stop at his favored café.

By now the Métro was beginning to fill with its orderly mass of mute morning passengers. An electric guitarist in patched jeans passed the hat around after playing the brooding theme from *Jeux interdits,* a classic film rerun several years ago on television. Kevin recalled watching it in bed with a cold, in turn dabbing at his eyes and blowing his nose, and he left the Métro with shadowy recollections of the largely unremembered plot, knowing only that everyone in it who loved had suffered, had been wrenched apart, and even the small dog had died. Not just died. Was killed by the Germans.

Once inside, his wet clothing now on hangers in the bathroom, he allowed himself some Mahler on the stereo, knowing that his personal problems would be reliably dwarfed by it. Easing into his favorite chair, he removed his soaked shoes and dried his toes with a towel. Despite, or perhaps because of the music, Kevin began to feel more balanced. He looked at The General with affection. The poor old creature seemed to be feeling the cold, tying himself into a near knot next to the empty fireplace and wearing a forlorn look in his eyes. Kevin then got up, stacked some logs on the grate, lit them, and drew his chair close to the fire. Now he began to take a more benign view of the soggy state of affairs and even contemplated returning to his small studio near the Porte des Lilas, until he was once again summoned by the ring of that instrument linking him to the rest of the world.

He answered the phone with dread. But it was the wrong number, though the man at the other end kept repeating, Are you sure, Are you sure? He thought, of course, that it might be Lea, or whoever it was who called herself Lea, and he did not want to begin all over again. He had worked it out last night; it had interrupted his sleep (and he'd had to get up this morning at a quarter to six), and it had entered his dream life. He did not want the question of her to remain tormenting him with appointments that did not work out and telephone messages that excluded straightforward facts. The emergence of Lea was responsible, he concluded, for these recent fluctuations of mood: his manic anger last night, and a sudden burst of meanness that brought him to speak so unpleasantly in his broadcast about the French. And when the phone call turned out to be a wrong number he was relieved.

But why, then, did he find himself toward noon studying the detailed map of Paris, particularly the region of the first arrondissement between the quai du Louvre and the rue St. Honoré, a ten-minute Métro ride, it seemed, from his apartment; fifteen minutes, he figured, by foot? Meanwhile, outside, the wind was hurling rain against his windows, and when he looked down at the street he saw through the streaked window a blur of angry pedestrians moving like beetles through a mud swamp. On the desk in front of him was the translation he had just begun of Duras' *L'Amant*. "Très vite dans ma vie il a été trop tard," he read, "Very quickly in my life it was too late," he wrote. Then he changed it to, ". . . already too late." He hesitated. Would the single word give a stronger meaning to the phrase?

"It was already too late," he said aloud, imagining all hopes and illusions clattering and falling into some deep well that went down to the center of the earth, lost there, never to be retrieved. He then placed his hands on the edge of the desk and rapidly pushed himself away, chair and all, mindless of scruffing up his carefully waxed parquet, and stood, ready to return to the sodden grimness of the streets below. He knew that it was an act of folly now, to leave the snugness of these rooms. And yet he knew that he must, for he had seen his Art Deco clock pointing to a quarter after one; the clock all at once so eloquent in transmitting its message that it might have been set into the pediment of a train station, vividly announcing that if he did not arrive quickly he would miss the journey. Would himself be consigned to the earth's cavity. Without having ever.

So much for his resolve and self-discipline. He once again fastened himself into his obligatory outfit of Burberry/ blazer/moccasins, and clattered down the stairs. What he had learned from the map was that north of the rue du Rivoli, as she had indicated, the rue de l'Arbre Sec was only two blocks long.

There were, incredible for any city but Paris, five restaurants, three café-brasseries, and one tea shop on the short street. These blurred before his eyes, for in the accumulating moisture his glasses had steamed over. He slogged along, glancing rapidly at each place, determined, as though preparing for a search-and-destroy mission, to get it over with as quickly as possible. The whole thing was a game of Russian roulette anyway, and he would give himself this one shot, going into one, repeat, one restaurant, and doing it on instinct alone. Here it was: Lea's big chance to meet Kevin Korlov, thirty-six-year-old American translator, teacher, radio announcer, and sometime sculptor: the Invisible Man drenched as a river rat in his watersoaked raincoat, his umbrella held high. He stood on the sidewalk, took a deep breath, and scanned the restaurants. Now moving rapidly, he put his face up to each window. One featured a publike interior, with beer steins hung in a row above the bar and walls covered in a dusty Black Watch plaid. No.

The following place was a straightforward bistro, well lit. Too well lit. A woman would never have chosen it for a rendezvous.

Next door, the small, chic room was on several levels. White tablecloths, rather expensive, judging by the menu posted outside and the various awards whose decals adorned the curtained room. Not crowded. Maybe.

Two to go. A Chinese restaurant. No. Not for a first lunch.

Finally, a turn-of-the-century place, slightly down at heel. Art-nouveau trappings. A bowl of fresh flowers on the zinc bar. Yes. Yes, without question. Now or never. It was the wide, tall bouquet of flowers that beckoned him inside.

He entered stumbling, alerting the proprietor who walked over to him, combining a Parisian impartiality with the customary absence of a smile. "You would like a table for how many?" he asked, not unpleasantly, as Kevin's eyes swept across the room. Several people looked up, then away. "I'm waiting for someone," he began, his eyes continuing to rove until seeing a table for two near the window and a woman seated there wearing a broad-brimmed black hat with her back to him; starting toward her, he paused, unleashed himself from his soaked trappings—his umbrella, his scarf, and newspaper—and thrusting these onto the unsuspecting arm of the proprietor while muttering something that even he did not understand, walked as he might have walked, half stumbling, when late for an appointment with an old friend, with apologies forming on his lips (although these were not apologies at all, they were inaudible cries of pleasure and pain and hope and despair); walked blindly toward the table. She turned and looked up.

Later he would remember that first instant: wide black hat that dipped low over the forehead but did not at all obscure the gray, gray eyes. A face so moth-pale that its delicate features seemed sketched onto it temporarily and could be changed at will. A brush of crimson defining the wide mouth, the slimmest of ballerina necks; then, yes, of course, the red suit bordered in aubergine.

"Aha!" she said, extending her hand as he bowed over it and rainwater trickled from his cuff. "So the man has made himself visible after all."

8

. . . . . .

The rain, washing against the adjacent window, veiled them from the outside world: together they seemed to be traveling on a ship ploughing through unknown seas. At first, Kevin was nearly mute, the conversations he'd held in his head throughout this period blocked by the sudden reality. But so adept was Lea at charm that she set about making him comfortable at once, chattering about the weather; the difficulty of getting around the city, what with the various strikes and political demonstrations; how Paris differed from London in all respects except for its rebelliously dressed adolescents who were similar throughout the Western world; and how wonderful it was that he, an American, had mastered the French language and inserted himself with barely a trace into the city of Paris. And all the while, Kevin could not keep himself from staring at her. It was not that she was so exceptionally beautiful—for her features on closer inspection were not easy to absorb, with arrogant cheekbones to give the oval face a tautness, and deep-set eyes that implied a profundity she might not have merited. He could not help marveling at her talcumed paleness, the particular chiaroscuro of her makeup (her carefully arched eyebrows above the gray mirrors of her eyes, the wide inviting mouth) that turned her face into an actress's mask waiting only for her (or someone else) to dictate the role she might play. As she spoke, gestured, laughed, it was as if some fabulist had created her and might just as easily remove her at will and make her disappear.

"But I haven't given you a chance to speak!" she said, lightly touching him on the wrist. "Where would you like to begin? You can start by telling me any one single thing about yourself. Anything. Whether you enjoyed your childhood . . ." She laughed with ease.

"This won't be a psychoanalytical session, I hope," he said awkwardly.

"Not in the least! But, you see, without realizing it you've already revealed something. I can now assume . . . let me see. That you are from either the East or the West coast in the States. Probably New York. And possibly Jewish."

"Just by having said—"

"Yes," she smiled. "It is not anything that would have been said by a European. Psychoanalysis does not often spring to mind here. We have terrible trouble finding words for all those things, for all those *self* words: self-involvement, self-congratulating, self-destructive . . . Well, I guess you know what I mean (I do like listing words). As to the Jewish part, one always makes the presumption that, as the Jews are—forgive the generalization—prone to intense self-investigation and recrimination, they would be the more likely candidates for psychoanalysis. Also, they are usually culturally minded and rather serious. And they would be given to this kind of exploration. Or am I mistaken?" She sat back in her chair and rearranged a scarf that might have been slipping from her shoulders.

"Well, I don't know," he said, in an offhand way, in

truth offended. His mouth was set in a line. "I suppose I must choose my words with more care."

"Not at all! The point is *not* to be careful. And don't go and sulk. Here. Give me your glasses and I'll dry them with my napkin. They are so wet and cloudy that you can't possibly see the food. Or me, for that matter."

Kevin Korlov produced a replica of a smile. But was able to clean the glasses himself, thank you.

"God knows," she continued, "I've nothing against the Jews, having flirted, once, with the idea of converting to Judaism. Oh, dear, I must have upset you in some way," she said, noting that his expression was so noncommittal as to be almost, well, invisible. Clearly, her charm was needed elsewhere, and she turned a dazzling smile toward the waiter as he removed their half-eaten halved avocados. Then, thinking to try one more time, she turned back to Kevin saying, "Don't let's begin this way. Both of us have come here—"

"—with hope in our hearts," he completed, with an ironic smile. Lacking a scarf to readjust he smoothed the tablecloth in front of him. "But so far you haven't told me anything about yourself," he said, relenting.

"Yes. Myself. Well, let's see. You are wearing a pale blue silk tie. I've been studying it, trying to think of why it rings a bell, and now I realize that it reminds me that I once had a pale blue dress of just that color. I was a child and very proud of it. And just before one of my mother's grand dinner parties—we were living then in Buenos Aires—I got an ink spot on it." She looked down at her suit. "Right here." She ran her hand back and forth along the aubergine placket near her waist.

"But that is an amazing coincidence," he said, some conversational dam having burst. "Just the other day I was reminded that I had a red tie. Bordeaux, really. From Charvet. You see the curious connection. And I spilled wine on it the first time I wore it at my gallery opening. I . . . I felt . . . I'd never bought such an expensive tie in my life. It was one of those extravagances . . .'' He wanted to take back the words and crawl with them into a corner.

"Well, as with your tie, I imagine, the spot couldn't be hidden. So furious was she, my mother, that she removed my dress—which I never saw again—and sent me to bed without my dinner (though one of the maids brought me some soup).'' She smiled at the memory.

"Why didn't you change your dress?'' he said in a measured voice.

"Because I was being punished. That was the way I was brought up.'' She took a sip of wine as though to compensate. "Anyway, I heard the dinner party going on below without me, echoing up the staircase. Each time there was laughter I remember pulling the pillows over my ears. I have bought many silk dresses since, but never of that color'' (and here she leaned toward Kevin, allowing herself to run her long index finger—nails far paler than her lipstick—across his tie) ''. . . yes, just that color. On purpose. But although the pale blue suits you, it is not quite right for me anyway.''

"Well, given that particular memory,'' he ventured, ''I . . . well, I don't know whether to be glad or sorry that I wore it,'' he said.

She looked at Kevin steadily, as though making a decision about him. It was now clear, by the way in which she twice tapped her fork against the side of her newly arrived *confit de canard,* that having tested him she was fast coming to a conclusion about him. And that it was negative. "The story is about me,'' she said in a low voice. "Not about whether you should have worn the tie.'' She turned her attention to her plate and sliced into the acceptable *confit.*

"Look, Lea,'' he said, placing his own fork, down on his plate. "I must admit that this is difficult for me. I've never met anyone this way. I have no easy access to charm. I've always known that, and I don't often put myself in circumstances where it is expected of me. So you can see that I'm at a loss. It doesn't mean that I didn't want to meet you. I did. Very much, though I can't easily explain either to you or to myself all the reasons. But now that we're here, face to face . . ."

"It was easier for you to write on the Minitel or to speak on the phone," she said evenly. "I can understand that. I think that is the secret of it all. The system, strange as it is, probably succeeds so brilliantly because it is a perfect way to hide. Particularly for someone who calls himself the Invisible Man! Oh, I know that many people tell stories, give out images of themselves that don't at all reveal who they really are, and then when the moment comes to meet, they are at a loss. Or make appointments and then are afraid to keep them." She saw that he was about to interrupt. But as she hadn't yet mentioned her most original thought on the subject, she wanted to add, "It's all a kind of trompe l'oeil."

"It isn't that I gave out false information," he had to say.

She leaned toward him. "I did not say *you* gave out unrealistic images. I said *they.*" And with that she put down her fork and knife, and dabbed at her lips with her napkin. Her whole being said, *Why have I come here to sit opposite this dreary, defensive man?*

"Oh, please," he said, reaching toward her. "Please let's go more slowly. I feel as though there might be something so valuable . . . You are so adept. You could carry on a conversation with anyone, with any . . ." and here, having to itemize, he began to falter accordingly. "Any head of state, any learned academic. I can imagine you at dinner parties. The seat to your right or to your left would be the most sought-after. You have that gift and I don't."

She waved away the compliments, her nails glittering.

"No, wait," Kevin went on. "Look, you asked me to tell you one thing about myself. Now I'll ask you something . . ." He looked up at the waiter hovering nearby and asked him to bring another small carafe of wine. He had already begun to react to the stimulating effects of the two glasses he had nervously consumed. "I want you to tell me what . . . what your favorite day would be."

"My favorite day?" she repeated, incompletely resigned to her anger.

"Yes!" he said, his exuberance arriving through sheer willpower and a new, passionate need to save the faltering lunch. "I heard this program on the BBC. Several prominent people were asked to describe what their perfect day would be. The results were really amazing." He was attempting the impossible: a Kevin all bounce and vigor. She looked back at him, mildly surprised. "You seem to be the perfect candidate to invent such a day," he was moved to suggest.

"Aha!" she said. And then, out of sympathy for the effort he was making, "Obviously, you've already given it some thought, have planned your perfect day."

"Me? No, not at all. I'm not gifted in things like that."

"You mean, you lack the imagination? How is that possible for someone who has chosen to live in Paris?" She now sat back in her chair. The look in her sharp eyes bordered on amusement.

"Well, I guess I can imagine a day filled with lots of pleasant things. Sculpting in my studio if I'm really in good form, or doing some other work that I like—a really interesting translation, for instance. Maybe some prose by Le-Creux. And no tension. Do you know what I mean? Only smooth sailing, everyone pleasant, skies"—he laughed—"serene. A walk with my . . . with the dog through the Luxembourg. A day like that. Oh, yes, and something terrific to look forward to in the evening." Grappling with his distress Kevin shifted his remaining cutlery.

"But you're blind!" she cried before she could stop herself. "And lost! With so many possibilities in the world."

And it killed him to hear it.

"I don't understand," she went on, heedless now of offending him. "A day, after all, would allow for so many specific, memorable moments, given that one would have one's choice . . ."

Kevin brushed aside the sting she'd inflicted, the accompanying wound. Gamely, he continued: "Well, I can come up with atmospheric things too, for such a day. Looking at the Seine, so spectacular at dusk in late spring. Standing on the Pont Carrousel, to see it—both in the direction of the Grand Palais at just about the time the sun is setting, turning those huge glass surfaces into fire, and the other direction, toward the Pont Neuf and beyond." The amazement of hearing his own tourist brochure descriptions appalled him; in fact, the whole cruel business of trying to communicate anything was winding him down. If he went on like this he would find himself adding, "You know, Paris: the Jardin des Tuileries, the Place de la Concorde, the City of Light."

He chuckled at himself. "Well," he said, eyebrows and shoulders raised, "I tried."

Lea was quiet, looking at him. "You're a nice man. I know men don't like the sound of the word *nice*. But I mean it as a compliment," she said, allowing him a wide smile. It was meant well. No question of that.

The waiter stood impassively at their table waiting for the silence into which he could insert his question concerning coffee. Lea shook her head, and Kevin said, "Oh, yes, certainly coffee." And in an aside to her, "I've drunk a bit too much wine. Low threshold, unfortunately.'' He did not (and in this he surprised himself) regret admitting it.

For a long moment they studied each other in silence.

''I'll think of something the next time we see each other,'' said Kevin. ''A perfect day, I mean.'' Then, unexpectedly, Lea stood.

''Are you leaving?'' asked Kevin, sobering all at once, immediately accumulating a fresh worry about having handled it all wrong. ''We . . . I haven't had my coffee.''

She looked at her watch. ''Yes. I must leave. I am already late, and I have an appointment in ten minutes on the rue Chambiges, which, if I'm lucky enough to find a taxi, is at least twenty minutes away.''

''You're leaving?'' he repeated.

''I must,'' she said.

''But we've barely gotten to . . . I don't know where to reach you. When can we see each other again?'' He almost shouted. From neighboring tables several heads discreetly turned toward them. ''You can't,'' he said in a near-whisper.

''I can,'' she said imitating his tone as the proprietor helped her into her coat while Kevin stood. ''I must. As for where I live, I certainly don't intend to keep it a secret from you. I'm fixing up an apartment on the rue des Acacias, a wonderful large, sunny place, though you wouldn't know it from the street. So like the French these days, don't you think, to disguise any sign of luxury?'' Then she laughed, a delightful musical laugh. ''And for the moment I'm staying at a friend's unused place, what I would call a rathole, on the rue Boissy d'Anglas.''

''I can't quite picture that,'' said Kevin, snatching at the bill just as she was about to reach for it.

''But I said that I would invite you!'' she admonished. Gently.

"Absolutely not!" Did the words slur together? Did he actually say ab*sho*lutely?

"Well, next time, then."

"When? When is next time? You must tell me before you leave."

She turned toward him. The full force of her—what else could he call it?—her *mystery* was in her glance. "Oh," she said, "the Jeu de Paume would have been perfect. But all of its paintings have been sent to the Musée d'Orsay."

"Yes, the d'Orsay is much too large for two people to find each other." His words came marching out in perfect order.

"No matter," she said. Then, as though having reviewed their conversation, she turned and added, "Goodness, you do have such a realistic mind! My perfect day would be so fanciful in comparison. Anyway, since the Jeu de Paume is closed, let's meet across the garden at the Orangerie. In it are those two immense galleries—"

"—with the Monets, the waterlilies."

"Yes, with acres and acres of waterlilies. Will they do? This coming Monday. I will meet you surrounded by those waterlilies. At three."

She briefly held his hand, turned, and again she was gone.

Your last name, said Kevin to himself as he stared into the plume of steam rising from his newly arrived coffee. I didn't even ask you your last name. Or your phone number. Or . . .

" 'The beholder's gaze moves over a surface of an infinite number of colorings, in which there is neither a subject nor an anecdote to lend itself to commentary. In his paintings, the flowers and branches are devoid of any immediate meaning, but the profound poetry of the work is perceived.'

This part was written by Paul Claudel, who visited the Orangerie in 1927,'' Kevin remarked, looking up, straying from the brochure he held in his gloved hand. His footsteps echoed as he walked closer to her, gazing around the room.

She waited for him to continue.

"Then he goes on to say, 'In the twilight of his long life, after investigating every answer that nature's sundry motifs could supply to the question of daylight in the form of colored assemblages, Monet finally addressed the element that in itself is the most docile, the most penetrable, namely, water, which is simultaneously transparency, iridescence and a mirror. Thanks to water, he became the indirect painter of what the eye does not see.' ''

Having read this aloud in his most professional voice, Kevin put the leaflet back in his overcoat pocket and looked over at Lea, who stood with both hands locked behind her head, as though deeply inhaling the scent of the outdoors. Surrounding her were the wide walls with their Arcadian atmosphere of willows and water and lilies.

"Transparency, iridescence, and a mirror. I've never heard a better description of—"

"I know what you are going to say," he interrupted, then paused for emphasis: "—of how you see yourself."

"But that is amazing!" Lea said, turning toward him and then crossing over to sit on one of the pair of velvet circular sofas in the center of the vast gallery. "You are not supposed to know that. Not yet." She arranged her pleated skirt around herself, fanlike. Her hair fell loosely about her shoulders. She looked like a rather grown-up schoolgirl, only marginally related to the sleek woman in the broad-brimmed hat on the rue de l'Arbre Sec.

"I'm not quite as dumb," he had to say, "as I look."

"We are the only two people here," she said, delighted. "In both these enormous galleries, we have Monet to ourselves. I would have Debussy playing in the background. I would have it rain outside. And I would bolt the door and stay here until nighttime."

"Would that be your perfect day?" he asked, sitting on the sofa, though because of its circular shape he faced a different length of the wide, wide canvas.

"Oh, not at all. Nothing so contemplative, so internalized. I must admit that I've thought about it since our lunch. My day, you see, would not be at all as simple as yours was. Quite the reverse. I'm afraid to tell it to you. You're so severe. It would sound hedonistic, I'm sure. An idle, useless day; no goals, no Good Works. But full of random sensations. Or as many of them as I could fit into it. Naturally, if I were to invent all this, say, a week from now, I might come up with another plot altogether."

"Depending on?"

"My memory, I suppose. I'm such a collector of moments, which is why I live so completely in the present. It's only at times like this that I allow myself to appraise the past. By the way, you said only a perfect day. But you didn't say a day that was logical, orderly—oh, what is the word . . . ?"

"Schematic? Plausible?" he offered. He would exert himself. He had arrived at this appointment with every intention of neutralizing the earlier impression he was certain he had made. Of a blunderer. "No. I guess the day wouldn't have to be plausible at all."

"Then I would have no trouble"—she leaned forward to smooth out a pleat—"in imagining it. Oh, this reminds me of an earlier time when I saw myself as an actress. What fun!" Then suddenly she stood and walked toward the opalescent walls and began to speak as though from a stage in a theatre or an opera house. She did not particularly focus on Kevin. But the long oval room sent him the sounds as clearly as if she were standing next to him.

"I wake up, stretch, feel the crisp sheets against my body, and although I am tempted to go back to sleep again, the sun coming through the window and across the table next to my bed is so cheerful, so full of invitation, that I feel no need of the safety of sleep. Also, there is a soft knock on my door and a woman comes in, a Mexican woman, without expression, a true Aztec, and she places on that sunny table a small tray with coffee and a covered plate of tropical fruits; then just as silently she disappears. She has not even bothered to look at me." She glanced over at Kevin.

"That would be difficult to imagine," he said.

"Outside my window there is a soft, rhythmical click, the sound of gardeners clipping hedges. I open the french doors leading to the pool and dive in, naked, staying in the water only long enough to absorb the shock of it. Then in a hurry I take a towel from one of the chairs, dry myself with it and return to my room to have my coffee. I am all alone. Even the gardeners no longer exist. My house is high above the city, though the city itself is of no importance, and when I am finished with my breakfast and am properly dressed I get into my car and drive down, down, toward the sea, and find myself at the edge of the three temples at Paestum.

"The fields surrounding these extraordinary temples are empty, and I wander through them at will. No one asks me for anything. I can clap my hands and hear the echo; shout, too, make speeches if I wish. I dig my hands into the earth at an outcropping just beyond the temples and find a coin. I feel it first, its round, pebbled edge. I pry it out. It is gold, the head of Demetrius. Demetrius, you know?"

"Macedonia. Yes. Conquered Athens, if I remember." He had not wanted to interrupt.

"The discovery of the coin fills me with a pleasure known only to serious scavengers like myself, for that is truly what I am, and in every way. But I see that the sun is high in the sky; I look out toward the Mediterranean and through the force of will I am transported to an island, where I lunch with a lover. I shall not tell you his name. He has no real name because he is a collection of lovers. I am speaking of lovers in the most erotic sense; I am not having lunch with someone with whom I share my life, or with someone I deeply love. We sit in the shade overlooking the Faraliglione, drinking our cold white wine—and, oh yes, there is prosciutto with melon. We barely talk. Our hands touch, our eyes are always on each other. We do not join the other bathers after lunch. We go immediately back to our hotel facing a square in a strange town, like Aleppo, and we quickly shed our clothing and, together, step into the immense bathtub. There we begin to make love; finally we are in a huge bed full of pillows and down covers. Awakening, it is midafternoon. He has vanished; I am free of him. I go downstairs and cross the square and find myself in a maze of souks beyond. I wander through them alone. There is Arab music and the scent of spices alternating with wet, earthy smells. I run my eyes and my hands across vegetables, across Moorish pottery; someone offers me mint tea; carpets are spread before me. I buy whatever I choose; it makes no difference: I cannot carry any of it nor do I want to. It is only for the fun of seeing, of choosing, of imagining these things in my life. My skin feels warm, all the warmer because of the cool, heavy shadows of the market. I have had enough of summer. The summer ceases.'' She closed her eyes and was silent.

"But the rest of the day!" he cried. "You can't just . . .''

She nodded. "I was only taking a mental breath.'' Then she laughed.

He settled back against the cushions, laughing with her.

"And all at once I am in a compartment on a train. I am alone in it with my parents. We have finally agreed to talk to each other with affection. My father removes his hat, places it on the rack above, smiles in a way I'd always hoped he would, and my mother sits on the velvet banquette and puts her hand out toward me to draw me close to her. As the landscape rushes by the window we talk about our lives, telling each other in a loving way all the serious things we had been meaning to say, though we do not have much time and it is getting dark. We stay there as though suspended in that railroad compartment until the conductor announces Venice, and when I step down on the platform I am again alone. It is almost night now. It is winter. The air is crisp, getting colder. It feels as though it might snow. I am now aboard a motor launch and it takes me to the Piazza, which is empty, thick with fog. The Basilica is dark, the amethyst lanterns receding in the mist. But the musicians are still playing. I run toward the warmth of Florian's caffè where someone waits for me. Someone . . .''

Without warning, Lea turned around, her face to the paintings so that they surrounded her now with their blaze of splintered light.

"And that," she said to him, "is my perfect day. For today, that is. You might ask me again in a week. As I say, my performances are never the same."

Turning. Bowing gracefully, her pleats surrounding her.

Kevin leapt up from the circular sofa. "Someone? Who? Who is the someone at Florian's caffè? What happens next? You can't stop so abruptly!" His own voice echoed throughout the gallery.

"Ah, yes!" she cried, raising her arms high. "I can stop anything at any time." Then, facing him, steadily: "And as you see I can become one thing and then another."

"Oh, I'm sure of that," he said, walking rapidly to be next to her, wanting to be joined somehow to the story she told. A wide, enraptured smile illuminated Kevin; she merged, for him, into the translucence of the canvases. In a quiet voice he said, "I'm sure that you can stop anything at any time. And become whatever you wish."

"And you? And you?" she insisted. "Now that you see that you can invent anything you want for yourself, what would you have?"

Because it was his turn, though he knew that it would be impossible for him, for he did not know properly how it was done, he tried: "Let's see. I'd awaken in Paris, and there would also be sunlight streaming across my bed . . ." He searched, he searched.

But she had the luxury of interrupting. "You really don't have to do this," she said kindly. "You are a fine audience, and maybe that is enough. For us, I mean."

9

· · · · · ·

Down, down, down he fell, his dream drawing him to some unnameable place; with his full force he wrenched himself awake just short of a scream. Covered with sweat Kevin sat up in the pitch black of his bedroom, his heart pounding fiercely in his chest, trying to piece together the shreds of the dream. Why now, when he seemed on the edge of some new happiness, was there this blind darkness waiting for him when he slept? Three times in the course of a week he had awakened like this. He lay back against his pillow, attempting, as though reaching up for a high branch just beyond his grasp, to bring toward him any images and memories that might soothe the sudden, inexplicable panic. He thought immediately of Paris. Ah, yes, Paris, its wide nighttime boulevards stretching in silence as he'd slept. He knew that if he went to the window and looked down he would see the empty, lantern-lit streets. Not a soul, not a car, the exquisite city caught in that moment when the death of the night and the knife-edge of the morning meet. He had, or was beginning to have, his Paris. He must always remember that. It comforted him, defined him. He was the American who had come there six years ago and, though never quite fitting in, had stayed. He spoke the language to a degree that surprised even the Parisians. He made a living. Less hair had accumulated lately on his brush, his comb, in the drain of the shower; maybe its fall had been arrested. His minor aches and pains related to nothing that might prove fatal. Having been provided with a modest nature, his needs, he had always been pleased to register, were few. He had never expected very much more than he already had.

Now he began to wonder whether there might be a deficiency in having had only these humble expectations.

Why had he so limited his illusions, always attributing intoxicating hungers, cravings, *yearnings* to others? In concert with the last of winter's chill winds rattling his window, he lashed himself for substituting inertia for feelings; and while he was at it, stirring things up, he turned his blame toward his correct, guarded, and scrupulously unadventurous parents, which they might have accepted as their due had they not been, both of them, so definitively dead. Having lived just long enough to see their lone son become—if not yet a full-fledged, functioning adult—at least not some druggy washout, or a criminal, or any of the other possible monsters that lurked in the shadows of society, they had managed to instill in him a protective shell and a decent education. Then, while he was still reasonably young, they had died in an improbable automobile accident while driving along the Long Island Expressway at (given their prudence in all things) unprecedented speed (80 miles an hour, he was told). As though in one hideous moment they had made up for a lifetime of caution.

Reflecting on his parents, he had gradually come to understand with a kind of affectionate longing that he had inherited—as most of us do—the very qualities in them that had always embittered him: he had himself become the most cautious and defensive person he knew. These qualities, he'd thought, held him together.

Kevin had accepted this, all of it, until lately, when cautiousness seemed no longer to serve. Now, reviewing at this impossible hour these certain details of his life and behavior, he was brought to consider the latest, most unexpected leaf in his book, Lea. He was dazzled by her—the response she must have wanted, since she apparently worked so hard at it. Every conversation was dramatic; every time they saw each other she had appeared to him in such a different manner that crossing a restaurant or a gallery or a street corner (the three times they'd met), he experienced a sort of double shock: that splendid-looking woman over there—who was she? Then the jolt, as he approached, when she became undeniably Lea.

What did she see in him? What did she want from him? His mind went laboring on: what does anyone want, he asked himself, from anyone? Other than to be appreciated, accompanied, loved, admired, hired, compensated, or released? If there were a few other things he was too tired to list them.

He switched on the light, felt for his glasses and observed the hour, hoping that his dream-haunted night would soon be over. But the clock face was neatly quartered at three a.m. Hour upon hour, carved in large ominous blocks of granite, stood in his way between now and morning. He looked around at his walls, he looked over at his desk; propped up on his elbows he looked at the dog sleeping in a newly bought wicker basket. He turned and lay on his back and stared at the ceiling, unable to resist these continuing mental exertions. He lay on one side, then the other, wishing there were more sides available to him as again and again in the blurred darkness he tried out the question of what she saw in him. At the very edge of sleep, so undefended, he decided that she wanted him, as she had said, as an audience to her. At the time he'd thought she was teasing. Bland as he was—

blind! she had called him—he was perfectly suited to it. The Participant and the Spectator. Lea on life's stage acting something out, which he would watch spellbound from the bleachers, and take home to privately consider. And with this thought he returned to sleep. By the time he'd awakened the next morning he had forgotten the purity of this conclusion, continuing to ask himself the question at random periods that week. He was to see her next on his birthday, and this time in the evening.

"But you must go ahead and open it. You've kept it next to you throughout dinner. Now you've put it there, on the chair, still unopened. Soon''—Lea pulled back her cuff to consult her watch—"it won't be your birthday anymore.''

They were seated in a café on the quai de Montebello. Dramatically illuminated, the massive flying buttresses encasing Notre Dame's hindquarters on its eastern, most spectacular façade were so beautiful that neither Kevin nor Lea could let many minutes pass without glancing over at the cathedral.

"It's always been a problem with me,'' he said. "I feel whenever I open a present that my reaction falls short of what is expected.''

Lea laughed, tossing her head back. This evening she had a gypsy air, her hair quite wild, screening and then exposing the golden hoops suspended from her ears. "I used to feel that way whenever I made love.''

Kevin felt his face redden. "I guess now's as good a time as any,'' he said, his fingers about to unfasten the bow on his present. He hesitated, then withdrew his hand. "I've been meaning to ask you—''

"Oh, *no!*'' she cried. "I thought you were finally going to open it. Oh, you *are* maddening.''

"—about the Minitel. I've wondered why you . . . I guess I mean to say, it seems so unlikely that someone as extraordinary as you would—"

"Would *use* the Minitel?" she asked.

"Well, yes."

He was watching her so intently that he thought he saw her begin to say, "And you?" But instead he was relieved to see her smile. "Oh, you're thinking of that first time we wrote to each other! Well, that night I was at the apartment of a friend on the avenue Foch," she said, amused at the memory. "We were like children with a toy, having just discovered it. And that night we cooked up the name Trésors de Tendresse, taking turns answering the messages. There were floods of them."

"And you got to answer mine."

"I think so. I only remember that I felt that you'd been badly treated by us, or by me. The Invisible Man. It was so touching that someone saw himself that way."

"You said (or your friend said) that you were looking for a very good-looking young man with a lithe body and not much brain as you had only one night a month to yourself, and that I didn't sound like that young man. Adieu."

"I said all that? Goodness, what a remarkable memory. Well, I must have thought it would be fun to say that. If not, I would have said something else."

"Like what?"

She looked out of the window toward the Ile de la Cité as though for inspiration. "Like, let's see . . . 'I am looking for a man of substance who can take care of my modest monthly needs, and you do not sound like that kind of man.' Or 'I am looking for an adorable adolescent to maintain in luxurious surroundings.' "

Kevin drew back, pulling himself out of reach of further

such inventions. "You're not lacking in imagination," he said.

"Ah, ça?" she searched in her pocketbook, extracting a silver cigarette case. *"Jamais!"* Only in French did it properly accentuate and conclude what she had to say on that subject. She opened the case to extract a cigarette, snapping shut both the case and this particular dialogue. He reached toward her with his lighter. "Now do open your present," she said in a cloud of smoke.

It was a silk shirt similar in color to the pale blue tie he'd worn for their first lunch. He was deeply touched by this and leaned over to kiss her, his first such suggestion of physical intimacy. She did not quite lean away from him; neither did she yield in his direction. But in recompense she smiled broadly, trilled *surprise!* and wished him, yet again, a happy birthday. Still, he felt rebuffed. Now, as he'd feared, he began to dwell on that same first message he'd just quoted to her. It was obvious, from various small signals, that her physical reaction to him was entirely neutral (while walking, she never took his arm; when she reached over to touch him it was to emphasize a point in her conversation, a light, noncommittal touch to certify that he was paying the proper attention). Maybe she really liked perfectly built young men with no brains. Why not? He held the shirt, still contained in its cellophane, and remarked on its splendor, all the while sinking slowly into the land to which the rejects and the monsters are relegated, dwelling there in the shadows. He looked across at Notre Dame and allowed himself mournful thoughts of Quasimodo.

"You will look wonderful in it," she said. "Your eyes," she leaned toward him, "are hazel. This will give them a tinge of blue."

Somewhat reassured by this, Kevin leaned closer and almost collided with her. But at that moment she turned and waved to a man who hurried past the café window.

"A really extraordinary man," she remarked. "An American film director. I've often thought how wonderful it must be. To be an American, I mean."

"Oh, I don't know. Why?"

"To begin with, there's all that *space!* We're so cramped here, so narrow in every possible way! Then there is the way you always come up with something new—even though your motives might simply be for profit. Take this cup, for example." She tapped the china rim with her long fingernails. "In Europe, you leave the cup somewhere and come back six months later and find that the cup is still a cup (if you follow me). Nothing has changed. But in America! You come back later and it is no longer just a cup. Someone has taken the idea and transformed it, while you were away, into a cup that collapses and can be put in a suitcase. Or has packaged it along with an accompanying tin of Earl Grey tea to be sold by the hundreds of thousands."

He watched her as she mimed these things.

"Or fashioned it into a porcelain skyscraper!" she said, her hand rushing upward until the shape ended, in a flourish, with an outstretched palm. "That is the way in America."

Kevin laughed, a sound both amused and bitter. "I don't see that as a triumph, though I loved your description. I always do." He smiled and looked away.

"Anyway . . ." she began, obviously attempting now to achieve something she had in mind. "Far more interesting to me is what you are doing about your sculpture. And when I can see it."

He leaned on his elbow, his index finger tapping rhythmically against his lips. "I doubt . . ." he began, then stopped. "The fact is, you see, that I haven't worked on it

much. I constantly reproach myself about it. The funny thing
is that I still see myself as an artist." He brightened. "But
I'd really prefer to talk about you."

She fluffed up her sleeves, rearranged herself on her seat,
and asked him why, why he hadn't worked on his sculpture.

"Oh, you name it: lack of inspiration, no time, no gallery
owner waiting to exhibit it. And no heat in the studio."

"That's probably the part that bothers you the most," she
said. "Paris can be so dismal and cold, month after month.
Where is the studio?"

"Ménilmontant, on the hill. Just off the Porte des Lilas.
I doubt" (and he inwardly cursed himself for all the doubts
he was expressing) "that you'd know it."

She shook her head. Clenching back a yawn she said that
no, she didn't. There was a silence. A bateau-mouche passed
along the river and its harsh quartz lights scanned the quays.
All at once everything was lit as though for a film sequence.
They both stared into the brilliance outside of the window,
and the great galleon of Notre Dame, deprived of its pre-
eminence, was forced into the background shadows.

"But that doesn't mean I don't want to know it. In fact—
good heavens, I wish those lights would go away—I've always
loved the name Porte des Lilas, and wondered what it was
like."

"There are no lilacs, I can assure you. It's a real working-
class neighborhood, a few rundown cement buildings from
the fifties, a few that are very old. Seventeenth century, I
think. It's on a hill. I guess I've already said that." Overcome
by the dullness of what he was saying, Kevin found himself
now leaning heavily on both elbows, his hands supporting
his head. The great arms of fatigue opened toward him,
ready to smother him and his sculpture on its breast.

She said all at once: "I want to go there with you. I
want to see your work. Let's make an excursion. Tomorrow.

I have a thousand things to do in the morning, but in the afternoon . . .''

"But it's filthy, I have no doubt; that is, I'm sure—''

"All the more reason. Are you free tomorrow?''

"As a matter of fact, it is the one day a week that I am.''

"Then that settles it. You can now drop me in a taxi at my wretched rathole. Actually, you can drop me near the corner of the rue Boissy d'Anglas at the Crillon because my idiot friend, who's loaned me this place, had her phone cut off two days ago, and I'm just in time—let's see, it's just about six o'clock there—to make a call to New York. The switchboard operator at the Crillon has known me for years.''

"Well, you certainly can use my phone,'' said Kevin.

"I absolutely would not think of it,'' she said. And before he could ask why, she was standing, gathering up her things. He picked up his silk birthday shirt and was about to put it back in its wrappings when he was startled to see that the inside collar was labeled Extra Large. He registered this as one might notice a thing in a shop window, in a passing blur, causing a turn in midstep to backtrack for a reexamination. Disconcerted by Lea's having so vastly mistaken his size, he found himself fumbling with the package while all manner of abstract thoughts about her mysterious behavior hounded him. So he forced himself to let it pass, following Lea obediently out of the café. Behind them, beyond the café window and the quay, the bells tolled midnight, and in a silent, startling instant, as dramatic as the sudden quenching of hope, the illumination of Notre Dame was extinguished.

10

. . . . . .

The following morning found a lean and resolute Kevin Korlov rushing through the streets of Paris. Off to Golfa Sport, the men's wing of the giant Galeries Lafayette department store, to exchange the silk shirt. He was determined to wear the shirt that day (in its proper size—medium—of course) without telling her of the exchange. It would please Lea, he thought, to see him wearing it.

The salesgirl opened the package, eyeing him dubiously as she extracted the shirt. He had been living in Paris long enough to know that this particular glance was a more accurate symbol of France than the old reliable *Liberté, Egalité, Fraternité*. Unmoved by the rancid discourtesies so often deposited at the feet of foreigners, he took a more worldly view. Still, he found himself discomforted when the manager of the department arrived, roughly of the same height, shape, and disposition as the salesgirl, and they stood there, scrutinizing him with a hydra-headed stare.

"When did you buy this?" asked the department head, clearly hoping to shrivel.

"I did not buy it," he said. He paused. They rustled. "It

was a gift. For my birthday.'' Another pause rolled heavily down the uncrowded aisle. ''Given to me by a beautiful girl,'' he remembered to add (this was *Paris,* after all; Paris of *l'amour, toujours l'amour*).

It did seem to have an effect. ''I see,'' they indicated.

''Look,'' said Kevin. ''If you don't have it in my size, just tell me.''

''We had very few of these. This shirt was the only remaining one. That's why it was on display. Just over there.'' The manager craned her head and turned her body, separating herself momentarily from her sidekick. ''It also happens to have been an extremely expensive shirt. Pure silk.''

''I know that,'' Kevin said.

''I do not remember anyone buying it,'' said the salesgirl in an undertone to the manager, who, leaning back to hear, was visually resynchronized.

''I don't have any idea of when it was bought,'' said Kevin boldly. ''And in any case, that is frankly of no interest to me. As I told you, it was a gift.''

The two women looked at each other. ''All right,'' said the manager, drawing away as she relented. ''I'm sorry,'' she said, though this was doubtful, ''but we do not have it in medium. This was the only one left because it was in the larger, less popular size.'' Now on her own and quite authoritative she motioned briskly to the salesgirl to put it back in the bag. In walking away her dignity was enhanced by the several mannequins in athletic attitudes manfully lining the route of her departure.

As he descended on the escalator, Kevin reexamined the previous scene. It disturbed him, its images were off-center, out of line, like badly printed color photographs in a magazine. Rather than investigate the matter further, he preferred to focus on the high-handed arrogance of Parisian shopgirls, to reflect upon the dour heart that beats inside this graceful city's breast, to discredit himself for not being more muscular and hence a larger size. But then he noticed a sign stating VENTE A LA CASSE. PRIX SHOCK. SOUS-SOL. Underneath was written: "Because our warehouses are overstocked with merchandise, and these are odd lots, we are doing the next best thing. Best for you! Best for us! We are not allowed to give this stock away, so we are auctioning it. WHAT DOESN'T GET SOLD GETS DESTROYED!"

Bargains always fascinated Kevin, who, although never altogether mean, tended (except when entertaining Lea) to be extremely careful with his money. Prudent is how he thought of it, though acquaintances often viewed it in a less kindly light. As he still had time before meeting Lea at the bus stop he took the escalator to the basement, where the "auction to the breaking point" was taking place. Here was a large, intense crowd of shoppers, a surreal cross-section of Parisians who seemed as riveted by the goings-on as they might have been back in 1789 eagerly watching the fall of the guillotine. In front of them, on a slightly raised platform, stood a rotund gentleman in an ill-fitting suit who was holding up a delicate, slightly damaged china teapot. On all sides of him were piled large wooden crates of assorted chinaware marked HETERO-CLITE: various sizes of plates, odd cups and saucers, and other such ill-assorted household items, some of it chipped, some of it dusty, most of it unmatched, awaiting their fate. On an adjacent platform was an enormous wooden bin, one side open for the crowd to see, and this was fast filling to its brim with smashed and broken dishes.

"What am I bid for this teapot, this perfectly usable teapot? Ten francs? Five?"

"Three," said someone, taking pity as he headed rapidly toward zero.

"All right. Sold." He knocked his hammer against a basement pillar. "And now this set of three cups?" He spoke at full speed, his words hurdling over each other: "Ten francs, fivefourthreetwo. No bid?" He then took the three saucerless cups and hurled them dramatically into the bin where they crashed against the rest of the broken china. "Now," he said, turning his energy to a box from which he removed a small stack of dessert plates. "These. Made in Quimper. Blue design. Twenty, fifteentenfivefour?"

"Four," shouted a woman standing next to Kevin.

"Four. Come up and get them. Pay the cashier. Now these three dinner plates. Three of them. Five francs? Four-threetwo . . . No?" With a mighty crash the dinner plates now joined the shards filling the wide crate.

Kevin stood there clutching the package containing his oversized shirt. The crowd had thickened, time was running out, the auctioneer's voice becoming more strident, more plates went crashing into the open bin. The claustrophobia was getting to him, the sounds of things brutally perishing. Now, of course, he imagined that it was himself being auctioned off in such a *vente à la casse,* lost when the original shipment was unloaded, or chipped, or unmatched to anything, sold to no bidders, heaved over the edge, and shattering into fragments. It was a scene out of one of his nightmares.

He thought suddenly, I must make her love me.

Kevin turned, pushing his way through the crowd and hurrying back to the escalator. Reaching the street floor he rushed past the ladies lolling near the perfume booths, atomizers aimed as they awaited their prey—none approached him, he noted in a blur—and fled out into the air where he was immediately entangled in the noontime trawl of shoppers on the boulevard Haussmann.

"It *is* cold," Lea said, dusting off the surface of a foam-filled chair, pausing, then deciding not to sit on it. She walked over to the wide window. "What's the name of this street? Rue de Romainville? How funny it is up here. If you squint while looking down the street, you might think you were on one of the back streets of a Mediterranean town. There are trees at the end where it seems to descend toward the sea."

"Oh yes, of course, the sea. How nice that would be," laughed Kevin, trying to disguise his discomfort in having her see this dusty place, having to show her his half-finished work. He hadn't realized, coming here on the bus, how ill at ease this excursion would make him. Lea, determined to make a picnic out of it, had told him she'd bring a hamper of things to eat from Fauchon, but luckily she'd hadn't had time to buy them. Lunch in the local brasserie would at least get them out of the dank studio. He lifted up one of the cloths covering the wax form of one of his most recent— though not altogether finished—reclining nudes.

"I often imagine the sea," she continued, "no matter where I am." She turned away from the window and crossed the studio to look at his work, walking in a way that made her skirt swing with each step. "The sea, a river . . ."

"Or a waterlily pond," he said, hoping to build a connecting bridge to those Monets and that glorious moment in the gallery. He noted that she was wearing the same gypsy-like dress she had worn the night before. This had surprised him. He had become used to the idea of seeing her materialize differently for each appointment. Had she spent the night at the Crillon? He dared not think.

"Your hair is very pretty. I like it loose like that," he said when she was next to him.

"A woman's face sometimes needs foliage," she said. "Colette, I think, wrote that. Or did I make it up?" She shrugged. "I think it is very beautiful, your nude. More erotic than I would have imagined."

"Do you really think so?" asked Kevin. He had seen the figure as neutral: a smooth shape suggesting adolescence, lying on its stomach on what he imagined was a summer beach.

"Very," she said, passing on to the next piece of cloth, turning to him with a questioning look—May I?—for which she received a nod. Removing the cloth she stepped back to view the statue of another bather, male, turned away from an imagined sun. "You've deprived us of their faces. That is so like you, to make a pair of shadowed figures, though I must say that they are beautiful. Whoever buys them will have to buy them both."

He shrugged. "That would be nice."

"Oh, that oughtn't to be a problem. I know so many collectors in Paris. Unfortunately, my family has a horror of anything contemporary. I can't tell you how many dreadful pieces by Barye we have. Men fighting with wild beasts, ladies being carted off by mythical creatures. Signed, of course. They always had to have things authenticated."

"They must be very valuable," he said.

Tossing her hair she indicated that their monetary value was something that ought not to concern. "And they're in storage, of course. But these! They're lovely. You have a great deal of talent. I know how awfully banal that sounds."

"Nonetheless, nevertheless, and however," he said, recalling his material on adverbs, "it is nice to hear it." He wondered whether he ought to show her his self-portrait. "There's this, too," he said, offering her Kevin Korlov in wax.

She studied it, studied him. "You underestimate yourself. In every way. For heaven's sake, Kevin, don't look like that. I certainly didn't mean it as a reprimand."

It was the first time he was aware that she had called him

by his name, and the pleasure of it took some of the irritation away. "I don't know that I would put it that way," he began, pulling the cloths back over the works he'd shown her. "I certainly have my doubts. Very few of us just hatch, full of self-assurance, the way you seem to have done."

"Seem to . . ." she said. "Maybe if one *seems* to be self-assured, one automatically *is*. If you *seem* to be an artist, then maybe you are."

"I work. I haven't had the time. Okay? But that's not really what it is. Anyway, I'm not going to play the misunderstood artist who's sacrificed his art to pay the bills."

"You don't have to play anything with me. I don't judge things; I only comment on them," she said sharply. "The secret is that you can *become* whoever you want to be."

"I don't believe that," he said.

"Well, then, let's just say that it's true for some of us."

"Fine. That makes the rest of us sound like fools. Right? Because we can't live fairy-tale lives? Well, I'd like to, but I can't." He waited.

"But you've told me you like happy endings," she said. Her tone was ironic.

"Are we having our first fight?" he asked. And then, remembering a similar bout: "Since that first awkwardness on the l'Arbre Sec, I mean."

He watched her as she went back to stand at the window. How could he explain to her that he knew his work would never be of the quality he aspired to, yet he could not bring himself to abandon the image of artist? What would he replace it with? There, of course, was the problem.

"I've always tried to have faith, to think well of myself," she said. "I've tested this capacity, without having meant to."

"That is amazing," he cried from across the room,

thrilled about such an apparently miraculous transmission of thought: Lea, too, reflecting on equivalent things. Was it in such moments as these that love most clearly expressed itself?

"Why amazing?"

"Only that I was thinking the same thing. Look, we test ourselves every day, don't we? From the minute we get up in the morning? I do. And how often I fail, moving through the day trying to figure out why it all seems to be passing me by."

But she would not be interrupted, as though she had come here to his studio to say what she had to say, having so clearly sensed his dangerous, almost critical isolation. It was a sacrifice she had to make to try to teach him something, become harnessed to him, if only for awhile, guiding him like one of those German shepherds as he tapped his way along. "No, no! Not just that. I mean life and death. I came so close, once, to dying," she said, her voice so remote that there might have been a valley between them.

He tried to absorb this. "I'm sorry," he said in a clotted voice. "I would never have thought . . ."

But now having begun, she could not retreat, she would have to tell more. Lea stood there, her agitation only apparent in the way her hands interlocked and turned. Her voice at first was calm. "Oh, in a way it's a good thing to think of. Funny, it came into my mind the other night, and again looking down your street, imagining the sea just beyond those trees. It always comes to my mind when I think of the sea. When it happened I was staying in Brittany. For a number of reasons things were not going well. You know, so often it's difficult to remember what precipitates a crisis. But I was feeling very anxious, terribly anxious day after day. One of my friends invited me to Brittany, to a small and pleasant town named Cancale. It might have been wonderful except that even in summer it was cold. Not only cold, but endlessly gray.''

"Lea, you might not want to tell me this . . .''

"And my friend said, well, I guess everyone said, that it would benefit me to go in swimming. What is the expression? It would be *bracing,* would help to remove the anxiety. And so on the third or fourth afternoon I did go in the water, late in the day. But I did not know about the changing tides. Why didn't they tell me? Something in the current changes all at once. Nearby, near where I was, that is, at Mont-Saint-Michel, they say that the water comes in and circles the island, moves across the estuary so quickly, like horses galloping fast across the flatlands. And so these same tides suddenly brought me far away from the shore and in a minute I'd become nothing more than a small speck way out toward the horizon.''

Kevin's expression borrowed her anguish.

"And there, with the whistling air around me, and the water, and the summer sky, too, so cold; there was a grayness that was as terrible as death. It would have been so easy, given my state of mind, just to have given up. But instead, I found that I was trying to swim to shore, trying with all my strength to keep alive.''

Her face had become even paler than usual with the cost of telling, her voice more strident. "The rest of it is ugly. Dreadful. I did make it to shore. I did, though I don't know how. A small crowd gathered around to watch while all the apparatus arrived, to watch me cough up the sea. Then the ambulance. There were days that I don't remember. High fevers, tubes attached to poles, long days pressed between damp and crisp sheets, between living and dying. And then there were a few visits from friends who'd misunderstood, thinking it was a failed suicide attempt. It was so much easier to see it that way, rather than as a resurrection.'' She focused, now, on Kevin. ''It was not a suicide!'' she said. Her eyes were now filled with tears. She put up her hand to push them away.

He went over to hold her. ''Don't you see? So few of us know this about ourselves. Know that we would fight so . . .'' By now he was covering her damp face with kisses, his tongue tasting the salt.

''But you!'' she said. ''Maybe you haven't noticed, but you're being carried toward another kind of drowning. Maybe you have to fight, too.''

''Maybe,'' he said, holding her tightly against his chest.

''Sometimes we don't see what is happening to us,'' she whispered in this newborn intimacy, looking up.

''Let's not talk about it anymore,'' he pleaded.

She pulled away. ''But we have to! You live as though fate had misplaced you! Don't you see that the Invisible Man,'' she cried, ''is the same thing as being hidden from sight, covered with earth, *buried!* and then, year after year— oh, God, what do they call it? They put in that terrible ivy that always comes up, no matter what.''

''Perpetual Care,'' he said, thinking of his parents and their prudence in all things and the sudden spasm on the highway when it all went out of kilter, thundered, turned crimson, glittering with broken glass. And finally the mottled gray stone so precisely inscribed KORLOV fronted by the twin barrows of trimmed ivy. ''They call it Perpetual Care.''

They looked at each other. The vacancy of the chilly afternoon had gone from their eyes, replaced now by a need to comfort, to be comforted, each for private and very different reasons. ''Make love to me here,'' she said, her mouth pressed against his ear. ''Here, right here. I feel so lost. When I remember awakening to find myself so *displayed!* Everything changed in that minute. Everything. I realized that I'd survived. But sometimes it seems so frightening to me that the line was so fine, that death is only as far as the open window, or a bottle of pills, or the sea . . .''

It was at that moment Kevin understood that her story was not true. So sensitive was he to her just now, so carefully had he listened to her that—as she'd insisted he do—he *became* it. Became who she was, and knew that she had not been pulled out to sea by the changing tides. Something else had happened, something more terrible, and in another way. Her anguish now hadn't come from surviving. The opposite was true; it arose, he was certain, from having wanted to die. Her sudden vulnerability shocked him, made her real.

He could not ask her about it. The strength he felt, the sudden untried balance between them swept away all the obstacles her perfection had thrown in his way. His fingers traced the small lines around her mouth. ''You need me,'' he said in her ear.

''No,'' she said. ''I don't need—'' But he stopped her voice with his lips and she relented.

He unbuttoned her peasant blouse and slid his hands across her shoulders, her face, her mouth.

''I'm so cold,'' she murmured.

Piece by piece he removed his down-filled zippered jacket, his shirt, his jeans, staring at her as she stood, frail and delicate, in front of him.

''You're safe now,'' he said.

11

· · · · · ·

He was in love, then, no doubt about it, skewed though the situation was. With its murky, mechanized beginnings, its idiosyncratic ripening, and, now, its erotic flowering, it was a land whose exotic terrain was of a strangeness unknown to him. And yet it was thrilling, though the rules of the place thoroughly bewildered him, for Lea would never invite him to her temporary home nor would she visit him at his. Because her phone was disconnected it was always she who had to telephone to make appointments. They met in public places. When they made love it was in his studio near the Porte des Lilas, still dingy, for they never stayed there long enough to concern themselves with it. Once they checked into a rundown hotel on the rue Poissonnière and made love through the night on the damp sheets and foul mattress, and when he complained that the atmosphere was sordid she replied that he must leave himself open to all levels of experience. It was the following morning, after persuading the Algerian concierge to bring them some coffee, that she told him how her grandmother used to have her servants collect violets in the nearby woods at dusk to stitch them onto her eiderdown, so that when she went to sleep in the evenings she would find herself under a blanket of fresh flowers.

Spontaneously, in the midst of a walk in the Tuileries, for example, or while seeing a film, Lea would turn to him, holding tightly on to his arm, and he knew that some other-world erotic signal had been received by her—he could never detect its source—and that soon her need for him would build (he could feel his own body stirring; after the third or fourth time he abandoned any attempt to shield the evidence of this in his newly bought, too tight jeans), and soon they would be in a taxi or on a bus or the Métro en route to his sculpture studio where before long they would be locked together, rocking and moaning into each other's flesh, hair, moisture. His own lips, he noticed in the mirror, seemed to have swollen, become smoother, and his tongue slicker, more agile. He wondered, too, whether his face had begun to change with so much emotional and physical agitation. Everything that was happening these weeks was in contradiction to the steady calm and composure he'd so carefully maintained in all that had come before it.

Finally, she relented—for his persistence to know more about her was becoming a source of small disagreement—and invited him to her apartment. Not the so-called rathole on the rue Boissy d'Anglas, but the splendid place hidden away on the rue des Acacias which she had been remodeling throughout the month they had known each other and long before that. It was not finished, of course. It would presumably never be finished, she lamented, but she thought he ought to visit it *en cours de travaux* with its furniture draped in cloths (just like his pieces of sculpture). Most of her things, it seemed (like his life until he met her, he thought), were still in storage.

And so here was Kevin, once again walking through the

streets of Paris, now in April, not quite rushing, contrary to that time—was it only just less than two months ago?—that he crossed and recrossed the streets near the Place Vendôme in a panic looking for a woman wearing a red suit bordered in aubergine. To meet her, finally, where she lived, or would be living, flowers in hand, a loose-jointed walk that was almost a swagger. Paris had conspired to give this event its proper due. The night, as he had hoped, was balmy. He had no real need to rush. In fact, he was early. He was almost pleased with himself: almost, because there was still something keeping a terrier grip of self-doubt on the Invisible Man within.

Several days before, when he had extracted the invitation to the rue des Acacias, he had been walking at lunchtime with Lea. She looked particularly lovely. Her dress was covered in a delicate floral pattern and her hair was tied back in a ponytail. Although he understood that her intention was to appear far younger than she was—rather like one of Renoir's pretty girls at the piano—the effort she had gone to (for him?) touched him profoundly. He had asked one of the substitute teachers to cover for him and left his class early to meet her, risking the anger of the department head. But he was intent these days on living dangerously, trying vainly not to care who knew it or what reprimands came his way.

They were on the avenue Montaigne, not far from the Rond Point. At the back of the Grand Palais the first leaves had dusted the chestnut trees with the palest green, the fountains seemed more buoyant than ever, and the constantly elusive sun had broken through just then (only to retreat within minutes, some concierge-in-the-sky offering, then witholding, its arrival). Suddenly Lea took his hand and steered him into an elegant shop, telling him that they would only stay a minute, that she knew he got impatient in stores.

"It's Porthault," she said. "No one has more beautiful sheets. Well, Pratesi, maybe. But that's in Italy."

The saleswoman smiled richly and asked whether she could assist.

"I need some sheets for a queen-size bed," she said. "Three pair, I think." Then Lea turned to Kevin. "Don't you think yellow? Yellow is always so cheerful. There's a great deal of sunlight in the place on the rue des Acacias." Then, without waiting to hear what he thought, she said, "Yes, I'd like to see something in yellow, with a border of white piqué."

"I have exactly that," said the saleswoman and they both smiled. Kevin, too, smiled. Spring, Paris, Lea, sunlight, yellow sheets, and this particular Paris, of perfumed luxury, made him feel quite intoxicated. The thickly carpeted store was like a private club, exclusive; there was even a curved marble staircase leading to further delights upstairs. Kevin did not aspire to this level of refinement. He understood that its existence, unrivaled, was one of the essentials of Paris's allure. But he saw himself as having been stitched together from humbler stuff, and the perfumed luxury here, he had to admit, made him uneasy. However, if this was part of Lea's world he would have to accommodate himself to it, admiring the scenery while taking care not to bump into it. Or think of it as his.

When the sheets were brought for inspection Kevin found himself agreeing with Lea and with the saleswoman that, yes, they were unusually beautiful sheets (that the cotton was a superb quality, the border beautifully stitched, and so forth). But when his eye happened to light on the tiny handwritten price tag pinned to one of the hems, he heard himself gasp, following this with some instinctive clucking sounds that caused them to look up, surprised, from their observations.

To avoid making a further spectacle of himself he sought one of the impossibly dainty, upholstered chairs in which he could place himself apart, exhaling and shaking his head privately, his hands dangling crosswise between his knees. During the subsequent negotiations (billing address, sales slip, signature) he tried to collect himself and not wonder about Lea's spending habits. It was not that this extravagance shocked him: not quite. But he had been thinking lately that Lea rarely, if ever, spent any money. Perhaps, he thought, she had considered it inappropriate to buy things or reach for checks when he was with her, that he would feel, as men are supposed to feel in the company of women of means, diminished. And by taking him with her to Porthault and including him in both the purchase and choice of this cascade of sheets, she was in the process of breaking down this barrier. That would be fine by him. He'd noticed lately that—particularly for someone as careful as he—money had begun flying from his fingers, considering all the dinners, theatres, movies, and taxi rides, and now he found himself considering with relief the possibility that one evening soon she might break down and begin to pay for some of it herself.

It was on leaving Porthault that Kevin asked Lea, for what he acknowledged was the nth time, whether he was ever going to be allowed to see this famous sunny apartment she was putting together. And in turning to him with surprise, as though shocked at having forgotten it, as though it was a small social blunder that must be rectified at once, she'd invited him to visit her there. Just like that.

"Of course. Of course, you *must* see it! I've been terrible. I'd no intention of shutting you out. We'll make it a festive evening—though there is hardly any furniture in the rooms (most of it, as you know, is still in storage), but the place is almost habitable and I do think you'll enjoy seeing it. It's so pretty. Isn't it a strange coincidence? Our flowery addresses? Imagine, you're on the Porte des Lilas and I'm on the rue des Acacias.''

''And all of Paris is in between,'' he thought to remind her.

''Ah . . . yes,'' she replied, rather loftily, he thought. Everything she was now saying had an unnatural, la-di-da ring to it, the first time he was aware of it. Simply by having entered the store and buying those sheets she seemed now to have taken on the air, to have *become* one of those *femmes de Seizième* with nothing but time, money, hairdresser's appointments, old husbands, and young lovers on their hands. As they continued to walk he found himself looking away in anguish, at anything—at the dog lifting his leg next to the lamppost, at the elderly couple attempting to assist each other crossing the street, or the young girl having trouble in starting up her Solex, pressing the pedal again and again until the motor kicked in—anything, rather than at this unexpected member of the beau monde who scarcely a quarter of an hour before had been a refreshing youngish woman wearing a flowered dress. But by the time they'd reached the Place de l'Alma Lea had switched back into one of those other selves that so warmed and fascinated him.

Lea opened the door, her arm elegantly raised against the frame. ''Kevin! Who on earth wrote the line 'mixing memory and desire'? We can't remember; we decided it was probably Yeats.''

''*We?*'' he said, surprised, disappointed. She was looking radiant, no question about that, wearing a long mauve gown that formed an obelisk of uninterrupted satin from high on her neck, enhanced by several strings of pearls, to her beautiful slippers.

"Yes, Edgar's here. An old friend. I've decided to ask a few people in. Freesias! They are absolutely lovely. Now"— in a theatrical undertone—"I've got to see whether in one of those open crates I can locate a vase." She took his arm and led him into the wide living room.

"Eliot wrote it," said Kevin as he entered the room. "'April is the cruelest month . . .' and so on. Very popular when I was a sophomore." He added this last on seeing Edgar, supremely tailored, who was rising, with an open smile and an elegantly extended hand, to greet him. Small pools of lamplight revealed that except for a few chairs the furniture was covered with cloths. On the wide walls, empty squares several tones lighter than the surrounding gray damask indicated where the pictures had hung. The boiserie around the doorways spoke eloquently of the refinements of the past, and of those days in the future when the room would be completed. At the far end of the salon a massive grand piano was contained in the deep shadows.

"This is Kevin," said Lea, "the sculptor I've been telling you about," and as they were still at the smiling stage they shook hands warmly. But Kevin liked none of it: the presence of (and obvious intimacy with) Edgar, the label Lea had introduced him with, *the sculptor,* rather than *my friend* or— dared he have hoped—*my lover.* But as he felt his jaw tighten, cordiality triumphed when Edgar coaxed him away from these unpleasant considerations by offering him a glass of champagne with a smile so open that in spite of himself Kevin was disarmed. Lea went off in her satin to seek a vase.

"We *are* lucky about the weather," said Edgar, the trace of an English accent further distinguishing him. "Despite all those romantic songs about Paris in the springtime, April can go any which way. Lea's been telling me about you and about your bronzes. Raving about them, I must tell you. I don't quite understand how all that works. The wax, I mean."

Having imagined the evening otherwise, Kevin's mental machinery, briefly short-circuited, jolted back into action and resumed grinding forward to try to meet these new circumstances. He would exert himself, unaware that along with this mental effort, a sudden straightening of his shoulders had caused some of his champagne to spill onto his jacket.

"Well," Kevin explained, trying to sound as smooth as the man opposite him. "You heat the wax over a burner and mold it, you see. It has to be just the right temperature or it can't be done properly. Then it hardens. So each time you work on the piece you have to resoften the area you are working on, sometimes propping it up with long sticks. In the end, you—no, I still have some left in my glass, thanks—you send it to the foundry and there they encase it in plaster, with openings so that the molten bronze can be poured in. That's why," he said, pleased to have summed it up and gotten it over with, "that's why it's called the lost-wax process. The bronze takes the place of the wax."

"And then they chip away the plaster?"

"Yes," said Kevin, trailing off.

"With the mold, then, they can make more than one copy?"

"Oh, absolutely," he replied as Lea swept in from the long corridor beyond the room. "And you?" asked Kevin, polite as possible. "I know that Americans are accused of asking this of a stranger when they're only three minutes into a conversation. But after all, you're already aware of, as you say, my bronzes. What do you do?" And here, glancing down, he discovered the spilt champagne on his jacket. With his eyes still on Edgar he began to brush at it uselessly with his palm.

"Me? I'm just a poor struggling investigative journalist," said Edgar lightly. Certainly neither *poor* nor *struggling* were words that might have been used to define Edgar, whose aristocratic authority was unmistakable. His raven black hair was combed back in sleek waves from his elegant forehead; his patrician nose was a vigorous refuge on a face that otherwise would have been blandly good looking: one of those too-beautiful-to-be-a-man's faces so often scorned, so often envied. Kevin happily noted that his ears slightly protruded.

"Don't let him mislead you," said Lea, returning with the flowers that now looked lost in the large crystal vase into which she'd hurriedly arranged them. "He's working on one of the most electrifying projects of the century."

"Of the century?" repeated Kevin, a shade ironic, despite himself still wary, still competitive. With a watchful eye he noted the flowers as they were transported, ever diminishing in size, to the top of the shrouded grand piano.

"Of the *century,*" Lea emphasized, as Edgar made mild sounds of objection.

"If he won't discuss it, I will," said Lea, gliding over to join them. Everything about her walk, her manner, communicated that she was long used to living in spacious places like this one. She delicately placed a hand on Edgar's shoulder as though to urge him on. "It's a book that is concerned with the United States Army misplacing an experimental vaccine that became contaminated." She looked up at Edgar. "Have I give it a proper synopsis?"

"Well, I began it as a piece for the London *Times,*" offered Edgar with what seemed a genuine wish to oblige her. "And the more I investigated it, the more horrific the material was. It seems the Army—your United States Army—was working to develop a vaccine against a blood disease prevalent in Africa and Southeast Asia, and they developed both the vaccine and the infectious virus used to produce it. This was back in 1980. Then, some of the vaccine got contaminated. You might have read something about it already."

"How?" asked Kevin, resigned, looking first to Edgar

and then to Lea. As they seemed to be in league with each other he might as well submit. And be done with it. Forget yourself, Kevin. Listen to what is being said.

"A good question. It is still uncertain whether this was an accident or whether it was planned. I've been acquiring all the documentation on it. It seems that some prisoners were injected with this contaminated vaccine to see how their immune systems reacted. Army prisoners—this was in Maryland, where they were awaiting their dishonorable discharge. Many of them were homosexual. Anyway, they kept them around for a while to see what would happen, and nothing did. So they were released."

"Not knowing," said Lea, "how their systems might react."

"You see what I'm getting at. The consequences are really immense," said Edgar. "You take a dozen randy soldiers, or, in this case, ex-soldiers, send them back to civilization for one week and they each infect maybe three people with the virus. By the end of that first week, we've got thirty-six people who may have been infected. By the end of the month you've got as high as a thousand. So far it is a theory, though many other diseases have been spread through tainted vaccines. But if this is true, if a contaminated vaccine was spread in this way . . ."

"Then you've got a plague," said Kevin.

"The Pentagon and the Army's inspector general have both insisted that the virus was what they termed not biologically hazardous. You can imagine the difficulty of getting anyone to talk."

"It is impossible to conceive of it," Lea said. "An error, if it was an error, an experiment that fails, and from then on everything in the world changes, can never be the same again."

"Astounding, the thought of sperm carrying death along

with life,'' said Kevin. He had been thinking of this in one of their conversations about the ratio of one thing to another and hadn't gotten around to saying it.

"Making love with the—what is it they put on bottles of poison?" Lea asked.

"Skull and crossbones," supplied Kevin, who enjoyed the opportunity of finishing her sentences.

"Yes. Skull and crossbones over the bed. Even tears," she said, "are tainted with it, they've discovered. And when one imagines them being collected at bedsides among those who are dying, civilization will once again have need of tear vases. Edgar, we must change the subject. It is my fault for having brought it up," said Lea, agitated. "Tell us about something else. The most recent story you've worked on."

"Well," he said in a patient, affectionate tone that implied to Kevin that they had shared many stories, "the latest article I'm working on is also rather gloomy. It's a story," he said with a laugh, "about carrier pigeons in Piacenza. Now, you wouldn't think there was much in it. But it turns out that after the disaster at Chernobyl half of them, launched from Marseilles, failed to find their way back home to Italy. In the orderly world they navigate by the sun, by their sense of smell, by the earth's magnetic field. And so when the radiation occurred they lost their way and never came back. Vanished. Oh, don't look that way. Listen, here's a better one: it has been discovered that an alligator's sex is determined by the climate in which it is hatched. Hot, male; cold, female. It's that simple. Certain lizards and turtles, too." He put his arm protectively around Lea.

"I hate death," she said, unable to tear herself away from the subject. "I hate it; it is contemptible. We are offered life. We believe in it. Then it is taken away. It is the essential deception, a gift given, then withdrawn."

"But it is still a gift, isn't it? Even if it only lasts awhile?"

asked Kevin, looking over at Edgar as though expecting him to ratify the question. A strong wave of admiration had driven through his anger at finding him there.

Lea seemed not to have paid any attention. ''You know, the first time I ever fully realized this (about the deception, I mean) was when I had a lover who died, suddenly, in a car crash. Two days after he died I received a letter from him, a warm and loving note written the night before the accident, just after I'd left him to go back to my apartment—both of us innocent, naturally, of what was in store. He must have mailed it late that night or the following morning before he got into the car. When the letter arrived it seemed totally natural. His handwriting, his particular way of saying things. He often wrote me notes. It reassured me that the idea of his death was fictional. And then, determined to believe that he was not in fact dead, I rushed to the place where he lived, ran up the stairs and stood at his door as though waiting for him to open it, as he had always done, knowing what his arms felt like, his lips. I had the letter with me, proof of his existence, that the death had never happened.''

''Look, little one,'' said Edgar kindly. ''Don't you think that each of us is affected in the same way? As a child the first night (if you'll forgive me for oversimplifying) you're left in a room alone, it is a death. Later on, it happens when a friendship for no obvious reason goes off in some way and isn't any longer recoverable. Death is constantly there. It never deceives us into thinking it isn't. By tomorrow, this evening itself . . .''

Lea put her hands over her ears, her gold bracelets jangling. ''No, I don't seem to be making myself clear,'' she said, abruptly walking over to the piano. She lifted its cloth, smoothed her long skirt beneath her and sat down, all at once launching into a Chopin Nocturne, the ninth, Kevin remembered, though he was startled by this music in the midst of such passionate death-talk that he could hardly believe it was Lea and not some ventriloquist mechanism producing the sound. Edgar, however, leaned in a relaxed way against the mantel and casually drew his index finger around the top of a burning candle to reinforce the shallow lip at the molten edge.

Suddenly she stopped. "I cannot finish anything," she said. "I never have been able to. It's very convenient. That way I always managed to deny having failed. It's a trick. Even moving from country to country or from one lover to another has been a kind of trick. Quit, you see, before I was fired. I keep reinventing myself, hoping to put failure off the scent, treating it like a mad dog. And I guess I despise death because it is the great, unavoidable failure."

The ringing of a telephone interrupted her. Lea set her glass down on the mantel, saying "I'll get it!" and in turning abruptly she knocked it with her elbow. As he watched the glass fall to the marble floor and break, Kevin saw that Lea barely noticed. She walked quickly into the corridor to answer the phone. The sudden image of the *vente à la casse* came to him, of the shards collecting in the vast wooden crate, of things demolished because they were of no further use. Her disregard startled him. From the moment of his arrival on the rue des Acacias Kevin had found the atmosphere unnerving, culminating now in the way that Lea turned, hurrying to answer the telephone, saying "I'll get it,"—in itself an unnatural thing to say in one's own home. And now, letting her glass fall onto the floor without the slightest sign of surprise or concern. He looked at Edgar, who seemed not in the least surprised by her and who said simply, "She has the most extraordinary view of things. But you already know that, I'm sure."

She returned almost immediately. "Pauline and Richard cannot come," she said to Edgar, "so that leaves just the three of us." She walked over to Kevin. "You need some champagne," she said gently. "When I was a child I remember asking a dinner guest, 'Do you want some more wine?' and my mother corrected me, saying that you never ask someone whether they want *more* of anything. It implies that they might be greedy. You simply say, 'Do you want some wine?' as though the glass hadn't yet been filled."

"What *I* want," said Edgar in a most friendly way, "now that there will be just the three of us, is to take us all to Castel's. We'll have a lovely dinner there, and there's the disco . . ."

"So we won't have to dwell on all the lives we might be able to live if we keep moving? Oh, I know I've gone on too long. You can blame it on the champagne," said Lea.

"Yes," offered Kevin, pleased that they would be leaving this disturbing apartment. "So we won't have to dwell on past professions, past cities, past love affairs." Emphasizing the latter.

"I suppose I ought to be more careful and censor what I say. But you do always ask me to give more of myself," Lea said, looking directly at Kevin. Then, with only the mildest curiosity she glanced at the broken crystal on the floor and idly pushed a few of the pieces together with the toe of her satin shoe. "Oh, enough of all this," she exclaimed, turning her brightest smile toward both of them. "Castel's is a great idea."

She then walked over to a cabinet, withdrew another glass and held it up, smiling, waiting for it to be refilled.

"One for the road?" asked Kevin. He had resolved to accept what lay ahead. And as he poured the champagne into her glass he wondered where the road would take them, for it was certain to be her road, not his; wondered, too, once he was on it, whether he would ever manage to get back to where he had been.

12

. . . .

The room was so still, so dark, so without any identifying illumination—no shape emerged, no shadow—so deprived of even the faintest thump or creak that he felt himself to be soaring silently through space. Or maybe it was a dream sequence, unfinished, and he was not awake at all. Or maybe he was dead. But then, all at once, from a faraway loudspeaker a muezzin began to chant: *Allah Akbar, God is great,* the melancholy strands of that pleading voice floating above the sleeping town, a pained, stricken magic carpet of sound rousing the faithful from their sleep. *Allah Akbar, ashadou ana Muhammad . . .*

Kevin shifted his weight and tentatively propped himself up on an elbow. The chanting seemed to have magically released the luminescence of dawn, for he now began to define the shapes of things in the room. Off to his right something glittered. In a blur he groped his hand across an adjacent table toward where he suspected his glasses were dimly reflecting the birth of this new day. Now, focusing properly, he scanned the neighboring space and picked out, carelessly thrown across the chair next to the bed, Lea's mauve gown.

He allowed himself to unglue a morning-mouth smile, remembering how yesterday at around this time they'd awakened in his apartment (was it only yesterday?), awakened to a grim, hungover morning that had inevitably followed their disco night with Edgar, when she'd finally, *finally,* agreed to come back with him to the rue St. Placide and they had placed themselves at each other's alcoholic disposal. But lovemaking had been out of the question. Staggering up his staircase and in through his door they'd immediately sprawled across Kevin's bed, muttering hopeless little unfinished phrases about the hideous pain of their headaches, the alarming condition of their digestive systems. They sprawled there in misery. No endearments had warmed the atmosphere, no caresses, no little words of love; only survival occupied their minds, and the great question of whether or not any Alka-Seltzer remained in Kevin's cupboard. It was not surprising that Edgar's name had managed to force itself between the various laments, his praises sung first by her, (he was, it seemed, an old, treasured friend who had seen her through good times and bad), then by Kevin (and he had a special reason to sing them, for he'd been worried throughout the evening that when it ended she would leave the disco in the car of her dashing, admirable friend—they made such a beautiful couple!—to drop Kevin off at the rue St. Placide; but no, once again Kevin had wasted all those hours in expectation of some doom that never materialized). What happened instead was that Lea had quite simply hugged Edgar at the curb; they both did, in fact, much to Kevin's surprise, as he found his own arm patting Edgar's tall well-tailored, manful back. Then she and Kevin entered the taxi and headed toward St. Placide. It was that simple. Home at last with her.

But it was only the slimmest victory. They stayed there, sprawled that way, and slept through the alarm, awakening in a disreputable state to a hideously bleak, unacceptably cold

Parisian morning. As though spring had never come at all. "We must capture it again. Bring it back!" she'd cried, her voice cracking on these first words of the day. And he, lying back down to nurse certain aches and pains, mutely agreed.

It was then and there, in the hungover gloom and misery of his bedroom with its faded faithful farmhouses and carts destined, it would seem, never to witness their passion, that they decided to take a taxi to the airport. There, as they said, their merriment building, they would board *the first plane going anywhere*. But The General! What to do with him? Given flowers, given francs, Mrs. Bomwalla would take him. Without question. The solution produced a burst of activity. "You get a vacation, too," he said, picking up the grumbling creature from his wicker basket.

Brushing her teeth with Kevin's toothbrush Lea had glanced away from the mirror to say, "But I have nothing with me. Nothing but my evening bag with my passport and my lipstick. And this *one dress!*" It enhanced the excitement, of course, seeing her naked, the toothbrush still in her hand, her lips frothed with white, holding up the haute couture garment he'd found so striking the night before. Her eyes were wide with mischief as she said, "Only this *one dress!*" with such a sense of triumph, knowing that such rashness was not in his nature, only hers, and in a manner of speaking it was her best feature; that she was capable of bringing him to it, getting him to agree out of the blue to take a plane, wearing jeans and a sweater, with only a passport in hand (and his cash, credit cards, license, unused traveler's checks from an earlier trip—when was it?—in his pocket, his coat slung over his arm). She was suddenly radiant. Finding a pair of scissors in his kitchen drawer, she simply snipped off with surprising skill the bottom third of her elegant gown so that it immediately became a peculiarly truncated, hemless dress, though one of some importance. "If it happens to be an Arab country," she said, holding the remaining circle of satin below her eyes, "this will be useful for a veil . . ."

"And if it's Scandinavia?" he asked, standing uncertainly in his nakedness, then moving toward her, surprised to note that though his poor, beleaguered brain was thoroughly muddled and he ached in most of his muscles, the most private part of his body had its own, obvious intentions and, despite his mental condition, was rapidly gearing itself up.

"Oh, it won't be Scandinavia," she said, moving toward him.

No, it was not Scandinavia. Admittedly they'd found themselves with a wider choice than they'd imagined when, before noon, they'd reached the Air France counter at the airport and scanned the monitor listing the departures. Kevin had—after all—stopped by the bank (trying desperately not to ruin it all by calculating what this wild, impromptu *geste* might do to his account) so they would not find themselves penniless on some back street. Though she professed to want to just go. Like that. With nothing.

They looked at the list. The boarding lights were urgently flashing for several flights, but they were prudent enough not to consider Tahiti, or Tokyo, or Bangkok, though Cairo was a possibility. They knew two things: it had to be warm, and it couldn't be alarmingly expensive. They were not entirely crazy, they each said, trying to reassure.

"We're living part of a Perfect Day, though when we first met, I never would have thought . . ." he began, having trouble that morning finishing sentences. "Remember when I told you about it? The day I invented then seems so unimaginative, now that I think back."

"I thought so at the time. Didn't I say? But we change," she said, putting her arm affectionately into the crook of his elbow. Her head rested briefly against his shoulder. "Maybe this is why we were meant to meet."

"Oh, this and much more," he said, leaning to kiss her. "Much. I feel . . ." But as their lips touched she was looking up at the monitor and she interrupted, breathing the word *Marrakesh*.

On the plane they ordered champagne, though Kevin was gentle with himself and left most of his for Lea to drink. At the airport in Morocco they watched, amused, as the puzzled khaki-clad customs official tried to find in their total absence of luggage something suspicious, something worth investigating.

"But surely you can see that when nothing exists," said Lea with a touch of arrogance, her hand drawing a large circle of invisible luggage around them both, "nothing can be concealed."

The officer doubtfully rubbed his nose.

"Of course," she continued, "you can search our bodies . . ."

"We have come here on our honeymoon," offered Kevin quickly, noticing that the officer was in no mood for her charm. "Having decided just this morning. And we didn't even have time to pack." He said this with such ingenuousness that it quickly registered.

The officer looked at Kevin, at Lea, and sighed, waving them through gruffly, with a flick of his heavy hand, obviously relieved to get rid of them both. Outside they were surrounded by a pressing crowd. Leaving Kevin to cope with the onslaught of drivers and guides, Lea strode through them toward the curb with such an adept gait that some of them mistook her for a film star (she did buy a pair of very expensive dark glasses at the airport in Paris. Paid for by Kevin, as expected).

"Sometimes," said Kevin, sulking in back of the car he'd haggled for and hired, "you ought to try being a little bit less sure of yourself. That charm of yours might not always work. One more word from you back at the airport and they would have had us closed into a room stark naked, our hands up against the wall while they took their time probing us with a flashlight. And that might not have been as amusing as ducking the press—which is what it looked like when you went streaming out of the airport."

They both detected a new note in his voice. Not exactly anger. A husband's churlishness. She shrugged, inhaled her cigarette, and leisurely blew smoke out of the window toward the rose-tinted walls surrounding the city.

The remainder of the day had pleasurably blurred by. Fatigue hit them once they checked in at the Mamounia—fatigue bringing them instantly to bed where in fact the sleep they sought was never achieved. So stirred were they by the sense of shared adventure that their mutual erotic magnetism gained new dimensions, and the third time they made love the final moments of it were accompanied by the sudden chanting of a muezzin from a nearby mosque. As though in acclamation of their virtuoso performance, these vigorous, atonal notes (recorded, as muezzins no longer bothered to climb those steep stairs) brought a simultaneous, languorous laugh from both of them. He had never felt so close to her as at this moment, so sure now that they would achieve an enduring happiness. And Lea, too, seemed in harmony with him. Though unwilling to express it, she locked her hands together on his chest, propped her chin on them, and stared at him with her cat's eyes, and he sensed in this look, and in her smile, that despite all her protective layerings she was probably as much in love as he.

Then, unable to further suppress their curiosity (miracle of miracles, Lea had never been to Morocco) they fled into the lavender dusk and made their way to the Djmaa El Fna.

"The Square of the Congregation of the Dead, to give it its rightful name," said Kevin. "And that"—he motioned toward the slender minaret piercing the sky, the thinnest sliver of a moon appropriately rising on its eastern flank—"is the Koutubia. Twelfth century. Named for the booksellers who used to have their stalls there."

"Goodness!" said Lea. "Then you *have* been here before. *Cheater!*" She leaned her head against his shoulder, having learned that this reassured him when, teasing him, she might have been misinterpreted.

"Learned about it at noon today. Typical of each of us," he said. "While you were deciding on which sunglasses to buy, I was dipping into the Michelin."

"But why didn't you buy it? The Michelin. Instead of scanning it at the airport."

He hesitated before replying. Now that their so-called madcap day was waning, the sturdy trio of clarity, responsibility, and good common sense were arriving to claim him once again. Here, cloaked by the oncoming darkness, almost as though thus half hidden she could not see him do it, he had begun to worry about his extravagance.

"Because we bought your glasses instead," he said, hoping this way to communicate something about money and her nonparticipation in spending it.

"Oh, what a pity," she said, stamping her slippered foot into the dust covering the Square of the Congregation of the Dead. And as he was about to misinterpret this, thinking he might have made his point, she added, "I have a collection of all those Michelins in a box. Tunisia's in it, Morocco. Oh, they're all there, the green ones, I mean, the guides, not the red ones with the hotels. And maps from here to China. We could have stopped off on the way to the airport . . .''

Kevin began to open his mouth, then clamped his jaw shut.

"Oh, who cares! We're not here to educate ourselves. I can tell you three things that happened in the twelfth century," she teased.

He tried out a smile. "I will be impressed."

"Abélard wrote about his love affair with Héloïse," she said. "And there was *Tristan and Isolde*—not by Abélard, of course, as it was Celtic. And there was the romance of Lancelot by . . . I've forgotten his name."

He hugged her for this. "You know such nice, courtly love stories. Like Kevin and Lea," he ventured, knowing and not caring how adolescent it sounded. She rolled her eyes.

"Well, I happen to know who wrote *Lancelot*," he declared. "But I will not tell you until you've been very, very nice for one hour. And say loving things."

"I am very loving," she protested.

"That is not what I mean." He took her hand and walked with her to the brighter lights of the Djmaa El Fna where the stalls were still open, and in the wider spaces lit by small kerosene lamps and small fires there were small knots of acrobats, snake charmers, violinists, and story tellers, all of them in full cry. With difficulty—planning on returning later— they wedged their way past the pluckers and pleaders to the edge of the square where, they'd been told, a decent French restaurant could be found nearby. Zigzagging through the narrow alleys they must have passed the place without seeing it (and here Kevin was reminded again of a certain anxiety-ridden search near the Place Vendôme that had taken place in a former lifetime). Finally relenting, they accepted the guidance of a teenage boy wearing jeans and a tarboosh set at a rakish angle. He also sold them a small quantity of kif, which they sampled after he filled the clay end of his *sebsi* and passed it to them in the shadows, where they inhaled it deeply. Quickly the kif exceeded their expectations. They found the restaurant with no further trouble, flying there on the wings of their combined euphoria.

"You know," said Kevin after ordering, "I am truly stoned. And why not? It is a vacation. We are not here to investigate the political problems between Morocco and Mauritania. We must leave that to Edgar."

"Oh, Edgar," she said fondly, running a finger along the stem of her wine glass, "a true friend. As you say in the States, 'When a friend in need needs a friend indeed . . .' "

"No, that isn't it: 'A friend in need is a friend indeed.' "

"But that must mean that it is the *needful* friend who is the friend indeed. I find that very peculiar."

"No, no! It is 'A friend, comma, *in time of need,* comma, is a friend indeed.' "

"Are you *sure?* " she wondered, "that that is the way it is?" By now they were both convulsed with the laughter they had not even dared hope to attain from the kif. "Oh, who can we ask? Surely there is someone here . . . ?"

His hand on her arm stopped Lea from signaling the waiter. "The last time I had this trouble was in trying to remember the whole of 'Four and Twenty Blackbirds Baked in a Pie,' " she said. "I only recalled that someone's nose got bitten off." She glanced up at the ceiling with large gray eyes as if looking for the answer. "But I never understood that one either." And again they were off. "I adore anything to do with words. Believe it or not, that is called scribble-mania. I know a great deal on this subject."

Lea's laughter turned to amazement when the entrecôte arrived in the form of a very small framed picture: a square, flat, ridged piece of brown meat within a frame of curly mashed potatoes. "Will you look at that?" she remarked, reeling Kevin back from some perch in the rafters.

"Nouvelle cuisine has invaded Africa," said Kevin, landing. "I shall return here to photograph this dish for Sasha Wittenburg. He will be pleased to have been remembered. I have much to thank him for."

Lea looked across at Kevin. "Who? My goodness, here I am, rattling on," she chattered, in blissful harmony with this man allocated by circumstance to her life.

"Not at all. I want to hear *every word* about manias."

"Oh, the manias! I recently discovered a list of them. A paramaniac is someone who takes joy in complaints" (and here she thrust Kevin an amused glance). "And a gephyromaniac is a bridge fanatic. I don't mean the game, I mean the span that takes you from here to there. Then there is the logomaniac, like me, just now, someone who talks on and on. Now comes my final one, because I am running out of manias. Though it might be inappropriate" (and here her laughter started up again) "to mention this, *orchido*mania does not have to do, as you might suppose, with a mad, impossible love of orchids."

"Well?" he asked, trying to steady his wine glass while caught up in her laughter.

"Well, I'm not going to tell you until you tell me who wrote *Lancelot*. You can look it up."

"Okay. I will look it up. It will be the very first thing I shall do when we get back to my apartment in Paris." He watched her for a reaction to the coupling of the words *we* and *my apartment,* but none was visible. "And what about phobias?" he asked, desperate not to lose the fun. "Fears are as interesting as obsessions. Lea, don't bother eating that dreadful meat, we'll have a sandwich sent up to the room later. Listen to these. I translated a paper on them last year. Take uranophobia, for instance, which is a fear of heaven."

"Oh, a fear of heaven!" She clapped her hands together. "Oh, I do like that."

"Or . . . what was it? Oh, yes. Atelophobia. Fear of imperfection. And there's another one. Kategelophobia, which is when you have a fear of ridicule. I myself" (and now it was his turn for laughter) "happen to have all of them."

"But . . ." He reached for her hand. The hilarity had made him—and, he thought, her—vulnerable. And this was a good moment, he dared to suppose: "You never manage to speak, well, trivially, to me. I mean those 'I've Got a Crush on You,' those 'You Must Remember This' words. You told me you used to sing songs like that."

She smiled. " 'And how strange' " (she sang in a low, intimate voice) " 'the change, from major to minor, Ev-ry time *(dum-dum)* we say: goo-oodbye.' "

"You would pick a sad one," he said.

"Oh, I was so mediocre at it," said Lea, lost for the moment in remembering. "But no one seemed to notice. I sat on a stool because I never knew what to do with my limbs, and in the spotlight I looked, quite frankly, like a bleached raven. But it *was* fun." She turned back to Kevin. "Anyway, one has heard enough of those songs, I would think."

"One might have. I haven't. Never from you."

"How am I to take that?"

More sober than he'd intended, he continued, "I mean *love,* Lea. I don't know why I feel foolish mentioning it; somehow in all this context it becomes almost banal. But there aren't so many ways of expressing it at all. Not nearly as many words as there are for phobias or manias. I mean, it's pretty straight stuff."

She, too, was now grounded. "That is true," she said carefully. "And if you say *love* fifteen times in a row it loses its meaning. I must admit to you that with everything available to me in five languages I really do not know how to say it, and mean it. And know what it means. It is something way out there, as far as the sea is from Marrakesh. Or as high up and beyond my ability to see it as . . . as the snow on the Atlas mountains. There, now you have two images that Cole Porter might have used.''

''I didn't mean . . .''

''Yes,'' she continued, ''I am aware of its existence. I am also beginning to be aware that you wish to hear it from me—though I do not really understand why a single word could change anything. Oh, where has the kif taken us? We were laughing so, just minutes ago!''

''Okay, okay. We'll laugh again. I'm just exploring . . . unknown territory.''

''Kevin,'' she said in an affectionate voice. ''You must realize that I am not here with you because I had an insatiable need to visit Morocco. Or anywhere else. If you want to hear the word *love,* I can use it, and mean it, when I say I love being with you. No, don't stop me. I *am* capable of feeling. How could I not be? Just because my life seems so fragmented doesn't mean that I am not affected by things, or people. I live completely in the moment. You seem always obsessed by what will happen next.''

''I prepare—''

''Like a good Boy Scout, bringing along his Swiss Army knife just in case a bear comes along.''

He tried out a laugh, reaching over to brush a lock of hair away from her forehead. ''I just need to know one thing,'' he said, and then cleared his throat as though about to make a confession. ''I just need to know whether you think *now,* in this moment, we might make it, might stay together.''

''Now, in this moment, I am with you. Completely. Does that calm you?''

He hesitated. "Yes," he said, drawing back. He fumbled for his coat and drew it over his shoulders. The restaurant was suddenly chilly, though only to him.

When they again found themselves in the dark alleys they were set upon by the ubiquitous baksheesh gang eager—*maniacally* eager, they said to each other, trying to revive the lost moment—to be helpful in any named or unnamed capacity. This unnerved Kevin, who said as pleasantly as possible that they knew their way back to the square, spurning the offers of more kif, the insinuations of odd and unusual entertainments, though the gang stopped short of offering him girls or boys as he seemed, by the protective arm around Lea's waist, so sexually committed. Tomorrow, he kept saying, and that possibility seemed to appease everyone. Tomorrow they would be at his doorstep in front of the Mamounia, flatteries on their lips as they proposed special VIP visits to brass factories known only to them, or mint tea in the muffled carpet shops of shaded souks they, only they, could lead them to.

But again passing through the Djmaa El Fna, yet another band persisted too eagerly. As Kevin began to swat at the nagging kids entreating them to buy, or give, or just pay attention, Lea, who had been left alone (why? he kept wondering), said, "The only way you will enjoy all of this is if you make believe they are part of the scenery. And don't take it personally."

Angered by their constant presence, angered because he could not be left alone to enjoy this moment without anyone nagging at him and pulling on his sleeve, he turned now on Lea for her earlier, inadequate *"I love being with you."* Rage, reined in, took over. Without looking at him she misinterpreted the focus of his anger and assumed that it was more ramble against the Moroccan kids.

"That's what you always try to do," he said. "Keep everything as scenery. You don't give in. You don't allow anything to touch. Anything. I am your scenery, too."

"Look!" she cried, enthralled, pointing toward a human pyramid just as a small boy climbed to the top to juggle bright discs in the air. "Oh, wouldn't you give *anything* to be able to give such a performance! And they're just small children, up way past their bedtime. It's midnight. So are we. So tired, no?"

Successfully extricating himself from a gypsylike girl who had placed her small brown hand on his waist and was working it, he knew, toward the pocket where his wallet was, he relented. "Well, it is pretty terrific, all this."

"Isn't it wonderful that we came! Oh, you're not cross, are you?" Putting her head against his shoulder in that way.

Which is what he was remembering as he awakened to the muezzin's chant.

13

· · · · · · ·

At the Mamounia's pool the idle presumed that this was as close to heaven as circumstance would permit. At least for the moment. At least it was as close as Morocco could provide. Fringed by palms, they found themselves in an oasis of perfection near enough, though far enough away, from the vibrating, intriguing town that in principle they had come to see. It was unfortunate that the vast profusion of orange trees adjacent to the pool heavily scented the air only at night, withholding the spectacularly heady perfume at dawn and depriving the clients of it during the hours set aside for sunning. The absence of scent gave them a little bit less of heaven, but one thing at a time, after all, and there were many other daytime pleasures anyway: beautiful models walking the edge of the pool wearing lavish kaftans (available in the lobby) and gold-dipped Berber jewelry (available in the small, lighted vitrines: *See the Concierge);* sun warm enough to mildly tone most skins without undue worry about burn and peel; drinks available as soon as you uplifted a hand to signal, and the pool itself long and wide enough to feel that even if those small children *were* to peepee into it, the sheer volume of the water would reduce their naughtiness to insignificance. Nannies, anyway, many of them quickly rented local ladies wearing haiks (but without the veil), were told to be on the lookout for such offenses. They stared fixedly at their charges, their minds . . . well, who knew where their minds were?

Lea was lying on her back in her newly bought one-piece bathing suit decorated asymmetrically with a sort of highway, a wide scarlet stripe running from her upper thigh and traveling across the smooth hills and valleys of her terrain to the very edge of her shoulder strap where it was obliged to suddenly stop short; then her vulnerable skin took over, so pale that one would have thought it unable to take the sun. But she was tanning nicely. She hummed with pleasure.

"What's that you're singing?" Kevin inquired, gently touching her oiled arm.

"Oh, so banal. 'The fun-da-mental things ap-ply . . .' " she sang closely to the ear he'd lowered toward her. "It's your fault. You put the song into my head yesterday, though I don't remember why. It could be, of course, that Casablanca itself is so nearby, though I doubt . . ." Clearly she was too pleasantly numbed by the sun to elaborate.

"I wish you'd sing a song from beginning to end," he persisted.

There was no need to answer. It briefly crossed her mind that he had lately taken up hanging too closely on her every word, watching too carefully her every gesture. Had she not been, at present, so effectively numbed, this concern would have risen in importance, but she left it alone and, though humming no longer, drifted again.

He had indeed been watching her, leaning to catch her every word. Nothing even resembling this had ever happened to him before. It was the stuff of dreams. His situation, even in the sunlight's brutal glare, was intoxicating. Having lived so long in relative darkness, she had brought him to this light. He was sitting on an awning chair at the pool of the Mamounia next to the loveliest young woman there (the anorexic models with fixed smiles parading flimsily by were not to be considered). She was sharing his bed, his room, his vacation: she was sharing his life. After two months she had practically moved in. Apart from several problems, puzzlements, hurdles (and who doesn't have these?), what could prevent them from—

"I'd like most of all something cool," she interrupted, rising on an elbow. "Kevin, would it annoy you to arrange . . . I mean, to order . . . some grapefruit juice? Fresh grapefruit juice?" Now her voice rose from its mumbling and, to make a point, firmed: "You always say that you do not know enough about what you call the real me. Well, fresh grapefruit juice . . . It is a passion of mine. A *passion*. I'm serious! And this must be the place for it. There are citrus groves . . ."

He smiled. "Oh, to reap your passion I shall put down roots and produce round, yellow globes for you," he said in the grand, orotund Shakespearean voice he'd once or twice allowed himself on the radio. With a jaunty wave of his hand he hailed a waiter whose eyes noted him and slid sidewise, continuing on his way with a tray. But nothing was going to spoil Kevin's day and he scanned the pool's horizon for another waiter.

"And we must not forget to visit the Palmeraie. Nearby. A grove of a hundred thousand palm trees. Unique," she added. This short interchange, covering as it did her needs, her passions, and her knowledge of the local terrain, seemed to have exhausted Lea, for after getting it out she turned over and flopped back down on her mattress to allow her back some time. But as she opened one eye at that low level, she realized that her every move was being followed by a dark, portly gentleman in black boxer trunks with a small pattern of dolphins (she was close enough to note) whose large-featured, somewhat cynical smile suggested, above all—what was it? Something in abundance. Money. It was a moneyed, generous face that had taken a great deal of pleasure in life, much of it, she thought, through the many numerals entered onto the credit side of heavy ledgers. Neatly written. And with great satisfaction. She did not smile back, however.

Curiously, which is the way fate most frequently operates, Kevin could flag no one down to place his grapefruit juice order, and he was obliged to go in search of a waiter. Odd, given the vastness of the uniformed staff. He didn't mind at all. He was getting fidgety sitting there. Besides, it was frustrating to talk to Lea when quite obviously she was in the mood to be alone with her thoughts, impenetrable as they were. And so, stretching, he went to seek.

"You must forgive me," came the soft words, unalterably in her direction. An accent. French colonial. "It is not that I mean to stare . . ."

"Then why do you bother?" This, a bit brusquely, from Lea, gradually propping herself back up on an elbow. Said through unsmiling lips.

"I know, I know. I study you because—and you are going to laugh—I am a plastic surgeon. Funny? But true nonetheless. And I have been trying to decide precisely what it is about your face . . . You see, I am confronted every day by the absurd wish to have perfection, to *give* perfection, and there have been times when I have achieved, well, something resembling it, though I say this in all modesty. What I am trying to tell you is that your face is far from perfect in every way. No, let me finish. And yet because of the way it has been—if you'll permit me—put together, assembled *by God* (I must assume), it is so original, that to get back to why I have been studying you, I have been trying to precisify—no, that is not a word—to make precise in my head the details, the relationships of your features to each other.''

''Oh, God,'' she moaned, letting her head fall onto the mattress. Then suddenly she was annoyed. ''I refuse to be copied. The idea makes me sick. It reminds me . . . yes, of one time in New York when I was asked to pose for a department store mannequin. A dummy!'' She flashed him a look of pretended outrage. ''Imagine! To be draped with clothes and plunked into a window. One week wearing a leather car coat ready for the Alps, and a week later entering a cocktail party wearing black velvet. No. I think it's best that you stop surveying me for future use and let me take the sun.''

''Please forgive me,'' he said, sounding surprisingly hurt. ''I hadn't intended to copy, for I couldn't. Only to marvel. Forgive me.'' And with this (she noted, through the screen of her elbow) he turned away.

''What were you saying?'' asked Kevin, trailed by an elaborately uniformed waiter whose babouches slapped against the paving tiles at the side of the pool. He had only caught the very last fragment of what she'd said, for as he came toward Lea he had barely heard her words *future use.* The remainder of the portly gentleman's share in the dialogue, ending with the formal ''Forgive me'' with which it had begun, he had missed entirely. ''I didn't catch what you said,'' he repeated.

''What?'' asked Lea, a new anger rising from her toes toward her knees and higher, its bubbles spinning upward, greedily ready to boil over and scorch him for his needling possessiveness. Her real *passion,* after all, was her need not to be superintended or restrained. Ever.

''Oh, sorry,'' he said, all innocence. ''I thought you called to me.''

Extinguishing the fire.

Once cooled, she decided in any case not to report the conversation.

"I was wondering," he said, after signing for the drinks, "whether we ought to take a drive this afternoon and see some of the countryside. Your Palmeraie, for example."

"To the sea?" she said, sitting up. "Oh, how I'd adore to be at the sea."

"But you hate the sea! You told me many times how it makes you remember that time you . . . well, an unpleasant memory."

Lea looked puzzled. "Me? Hate the *sea? Never!*" Then, as she reached for her grapefruit juice (tinned, obviously; not Kevin's fault), she corrected herself: "Ah! The sea in Brittany! The *northern* sea! Indeed I hate it. So gray and menacing. But here in this Mediterranean brilliance, all is benign."

He watched, fascinated, as she maneuvered from sea to sea. How adept she was at performance, ending it always with a dazzling smile. The recurrent impulse to howl *Why must you invent?* was choked back once again. He could not risk ruining the day.

"I'd thought we'd drive into the Atlas. Toward Ouarzazate. In time to return for dinner. Maybe about a hundred and fifty kilometers. After all, how often do we come to Morocco?" He aimed only to please.

"You are restless," she said.

"Well," he said, looking humbly at his naked toes, "I burn."

There was, inevitably, a second, fleeting encounter with the dark man, and this occurred once again in Kevin's absence, while he was arranging the rental of a car with the concierge. It was an elegant exchange, mid-carpet, in the newly refurbished lobby, an effort that forever obliterated the lobby's original darkness and mystery and intrigue, the elements that singularized the hotel in the first place, luring from far and wide its dark and mysterious and intriguing guests (now extinct). Yet there was this portly man. And taller than she had thought.

It was Lea who spoke first. She was wearing her mauve cut-off dress, newly pressed, using the lower portion now as a scarf. The effect on her was quite stylish. "I hadn't meant to be rude earlier," she allowed. "You touched a nerve, I suppose."

"Which is what a plastic surgeon must avoid at all costs. One touched nerve and all my clients who come to me on the Côte d'Ivoire would hear of it and take their business to my competitor in Rio." He had not smiled as yet.

"The Côte d'Ivoire?" she said, now curious. "Such a name for a country! I've always imagined it as a place carved out in pleats, facing the sea, veined and slightly yellowing. Oh, and with turrets. Silver turrets."

"You will be disappointed, madame," he said. "It looks rather like a cross between Miami and Tel Aviv. Cement skyscrapers. Oil. The most expensive place in Africa. To be avoided." He smiled and held out his card. "Unless one has a reason to be there." He bowed slightly and moved away. "In any case," he said, looking back at her, then glancing down, "you're practically standing on it."

Lea followed his glance, and at her feet discovered that the central motif of the carpet was a vast map of Africa. The lobby, pinkly dark, required her to look hard to locate where she was. L'Afrique Equatoriale, she saw, spelled out in gold pile. She stood at the equator itself; above it she found Nigeria. She turned, following the coast. Côte d'Or, it said, then Côte d'Ivoire.

"You look so funny!" Kevin called as he came in from

the brilliant sunlight, "like a cat chasing its tail." And as he said this, he walked toward her to see what she saw; his foot caught on the edge of the Continent of Africa carpet and he tripped, there in the center of the lobby, slightly above the Sahara, his arms going this way and that, clutching at air as his maps, brochures, passport, car papers, and car keys flung themselves toward the Belgian Congo, toward Khartoum, toward the shores of the Mediterranean and the Persian Gulf, and all the places he could never visit in a lifetime. As Lea watched, she felt herself grappling with an internal howl of laughter that built, built, nearly suffocating her. Rushing toward Kevin on dainty steps, she was blocked by his waving her away, his saying absurdly, "No, I'm perfectly all right," and trying to rise in sections. Was there space enough inside her to contain her colossal, indecent laughter? She thought that her head might burst, though little did the giggling demons and djinns inside her care one way or the other. She wobbled, managing to say through lips barely open, "Are you sure?" but only just, while her wretched mind played back the vaudeville scene once again.

"I think I might have broken . . . no, sprained. Yes, either sprained or strained my ankle. Oh, God, what *pain!*" He rose with difficulty, hobbling to a chair, his hobble, such an old man's gait, allowing a moment's tenderness to force its way in through the seams of her laughter, controlling it, even taking some of it away. For which she was most grateful.

Though not all of it. Further comedy was due. After the papers and keys and documents had been picked up by scurrying bellboys, the very doctor who had so courteously handed madame his card just moments before had, hearing the commotion, turned back, and it was he, of all people, who assured Mr. and Mrs.—What? Oh, excuse me—Mr. Korlov and, ah yes, mademoiselle, that happily it was just a

strain, not a sprain, and though painful it was only temporary. No, an X-ray wouldn't do any harm.

"And if there is anything else you might need (though
this is a bit out of my line)," he completed, "I am here for
the remainder of the week." Kevin properly shook his hand
and muttered how grateful, and the doctor was smiled on his
way by her, a smile close to bursting. A madwoman's smile,
he might have thought if he hadn't understood it.

And it was when she went out to locate the car in the
parking lot, for now it was she who would drive (it was his
right foot, wouldn't you know, the one that worked the gas
pedal), that she collapsed at the wheel and, in the awful heat
of the closed car, rocked with uncontained hysteria. But minutes later—as her habit was to vault effortlessly from thing to
thing—she drove up under the canopy composed and solici-
tous, her mauve scarf fluttering just so, as he was helped,
muttering, by the oh-so-careful staff into the front seat next
to her, and away they drove, her foot astonishingly sure on
the accelerator as the speedometer swiftly rose.

Soon they were in the open countryside; the sun, still hot,
bringing up a mirage each time they ascended, the road ahead
always holding a pool of water at its farthest point; offering,
then failing again and again to provide it, as the road wound
on, a gray-white ribbon stretched across the rubbly rose. Now
and then small packs of boys or girls would leap over the
brush adjacent to the road and offer crystals of amethyst,
unexpectedly the same hue as the hills. They slowed down
and pulled the car to the side once, thinking to buy, and were
besieged by another pack of similar children, who rose above
the scrub brush with similar wares and similar hopes.

"We can't buy them all, so we'd better not buy any,"
said Kevin regretfully, urging Lea to drive on. She maintained her silence, not caring much about the amethysts or
the children who sold them, pleased, thrilled, in fact, to be

in motion. Fast motion, too, and it was a wonder, as she said later, that Kevin didn't wear a hole in the rubber carpet where he'd installed his imaginary brake.

In almost no time they'd gone over a hundred kilometers and at the same moment the sun had lost its strength, a chill filled the air, and a great shadow was throwing itself over the landscape and over them. Until that sudden dark conspiracy of external and internal melancholy, they had been gossiping away and were still filled with a sense, no matter how modest, of adventure.

"Are you sure you want to turn back," she inquired, "before the dark sets in?"

"Well, I see nothing ahead. Nothing nearby. Not enough to make it worthwhile." He was holding his green Michelin, bought anyway at the hotel desk.

"Oh, the word worth*while!* How I loathe it," she began in a tone. But they both let it pass.

"You're being really good, to be stuck with the driving," he said, not for the first or second time.

And she replied, as she had, "You don't seem to understand that I *love* to drive. If I'd been a man (and I bitterly regret not having had the opportunity, at least for a while) I'd have taken up racing. Do you know I was brought as a small girl to Le Mans on the day the silver Porsche left the track and shot into the crowd, decapitating I can't remember how many in the grandstand? Dreadful. Dreadful. I barely understood what had happened. And yet I still love racing."

"Well, you're a pretty tough cookie," he said lightly, reaching toward her. "But you do speak often of death."

She decided to take it well. "All people in love with life do."

"I don't share that impression."

"I've come closer than you, perhaps, or more often. Oh, look, they're *still* selling amethysts. How many hours they must spend at the side of the road waiting for someone to buy! Or searching for the stones."

"So few cars pass. They can't make more than a few dollars. If that," he said, guilty for the way, earlier, he'd brushed them aside. "Maybe we should have bought some after all. Amethyst, though—isn't that supposed to be an unlucky stone? Or is it opal?"

She shrugged. "Anyway, it's funny that you have said that about death, because I have been thinking . . ." She motioned toward the stark hills paralleling the road. "Remembering a similar mountainside, though covered in deep snow. But the same craggy face, and like this, not many trees. It was on a skiing holiday at Megève. Typically I'd gone off by myself, so sure I was that I could make my own way, my own tracks. But coming down a steep pass I fell."

"The way I fell in the lobby? That must have been a sight," he said quickly, propelled by an overwhelming determination to change the subject, sensing that a catastrophe thundered in the near distance. The road would be torn from under them. The mountain would heave up and come crashing down. He forced himself to chuckle, and looked down at his foot. "I can't ever stop myself from laughing when I see someone fall. You were awfully good about it. And lucky that doctor happened by."

"Oh, there's always someone who . . . who comes along." Staring ahead, she withdrew a cigarette and held it, waiting for it to be lit.

Kevin did not see the expression on her face, the mask of resignation that tightened her features, hardened them as though she had been condemned and sentenced by what she'd just said.

"Anyway, I was falling swiftly down the side of a hill, skis ripped off, tumbling and turning, when I realized, when I *understood* that the hill had an edge. The deep snow suddenly ended ahead, and there, below it, in a drop of, oh, I don't know, five hundred meters, was Megève, like a tiny town in a department store window at Christmas. That toy-like. That far away. Nothing could stop my fall. Nothing! My arms had lives of their own, grasping at the stones, the boulders, at anything I passed. And in the end I was saved by three or four branches. Green branches that bent and did not snap, slim, the size of mountain laurel or wild berries—branches still alive under the snow. My"—she looked down at her hand holding the wheel—"my fingers, by themselves, felt them as they slid past, and closed over them, holding me there. And saved me."

Kevin could never explain to himself what followed next. It came, he knew, from an accumulation of these swiftly told, impromptu stories, in restaurants and on walks, even in bed, just after making love. All of her memories—if they were memories—were spellbinding, particularly to one so caught up in adoration as he. And it was not that his feeling at this moment had slackened. But at that hour, the sun dying behind the massive Atlas, and the cold, and the unknown place, and the fact that he did not want to hear of Le Mans or Megève; instead, in a sudden spasm of loneliness he required a touch, or to catch her glance and find it loving. He had not expected to say:

"I would really not like to hear any more stories. Whether they are true stories or fantasies. Not for a while."

She glanced over at him.

Agitated by the pressure building inside him, he went on. "We're driving through Morocco together, and that's all I care to think about now. The present moment. Just as you told me I should. I don't want to think of it as an anecdote you will tell at another time. No more stories of past triumphs. No sports car rallies, no brushes with death."

Lea opened her mouth to speak. But no sound came. He

reached over for her hand. "I'm in love with you, Lea. You must know that."

She said, finally, "I simply cannot manage the depths of feeling you require of me."

"There's no reason—"

"There is every reason. I told you that I can't manage it. We spend lifetimes avoiding things that we cannot manage. Look at how we deny that time is passing! Watch how women behave in beauty parlors, or in department stores when they try on dresses. Or how men look at themselves in car mirrors when they stop at a traffic light and believe themselves unobserved. They re-create!"

"I'm trying to talk about us. Not about people looking into mirrors."

"Us? We come from different universes. You can't expect me to surrender to your solidity, your reasonableness. I can't. Just as you can't—"

"Soar?"

"Yes. Fine. You've understood."

He could say nothing. The waning sunlight lit them both cruelly. He turned back to look at the road.

And then, in the silence, he said loudly, "I'd hoped that we . . . I wanted us to talk about what happens when we've left Morocco, when we get back to real life. I want us to—"

She glanced quickly at him, not wanting to hear the rest. "Of *real life!* How do you make the distinction, you who claim to love fables and myths?" she interrupted, so anxious was she now not to listen to any more: not to hear about his feelings, or to talk about love, or their future together, which is where she knew, had feared, that it was all inevitably, disastrously heading. And to avoid falling farther she grasped, as in her story, at a branch that bent. But then snapped: "Do you want a nice, tame example of how it works, how easily even *you,* with your determination to—as you say—stick to the facts, how even *you* avoid being trapped into reality?''

"No!" he shouted, his anger rising. "Why do you tell me stories? I want to talk about the two of us."

"The two of us? Well, this is about us. Yes, listen. I thought of it last night when we were together, when we stood with that boy smoking kif and we both caught sight of those dripping calves' heads in the butcher's stall, and that pile of small, bloodied hooves and broken horns. I saw you turn instantly away, as I did; in fact we moved quickly around the corner and went to dinner, making believe we hadn't seen, noticing instead the pretty skeins of dyed wool in bright colors drying above us on wires—No, don't stop me—In the same way we can go on inventing—''

"Lea, why are you doing this?" he said.

"We denied what we couldn't manage! I'm trying to teach you about illusion," she said. "Once you understand where it starts, you realize that it can lead you anywhere."

"Don't teach me!" he shouted. *"Love me!"* The cry was so loud that she was terrified.

And then, an instant later, at the same pitch: *"Lea, be careful, for Christ's sake,"* grinding his sole into the invisible brake. Along the roadside was yet another child selling amethysts, leaping up from the gully that separated the scrub growth from the road, holding the crystals high to catch the very last of the sun. And in a panic because he'd shouted so, Lea turned her wheel, braked; the car, signaled incorrectly, swerved and picked up the child as a mother animal might have, dragging it alongside the road, the amethyst crystals splintering the windshield.

14

. . . .

"All right, all right!" he said aloud, turning around and around the room and then walking over to the small window, his hands fluttering like windmills. He was alone. He knew that he was talking to himself and moving around stooped under the low ceiling like someone crazed. But in this he felt the promise of a release, the way people are said to keen and wail over a death and thus exorcise their grief. Through the grilled window, placed high, just at the edge of the dwarf ceiling, he looked at the surrounding hills bathed in moonlight, and for a moment he tried to let the purity of the African night take over and enter him.

But his mind went toiling on, crossing and recrossing the same tracks until they were grooved into his cells and marrow and had become part of him.

If only the stars . . . He took a handkerchief from his pocket, removed his glasses, exhaled against the lenses and rubbed them; the sound of his own small breath surprised him. Comforted him.

If only the stars would line up the way he knew them he might find his familiar constellations.

He blamed himself. He blamed himself for everything that had happened. Such blame had nurtured him all his life, lived, breathed within him like a private serpent under the skin. Now the image came to him, a rag-wrapped bundle at the side of the road instantly transforming itself into a Berber girl, her yellowish limbs angled against her body. In the first moments of panic he was sure she was dead; her eyes were lifeless, a bubble clotted one nostril. He leaned over her, his hands trembling. As though emerging from a dream she suddenly screamed and clawed at the air. He jumped back as she tried to stand. But her legs would not support her. *"Reste. Reste ici."* He said, trying to calm her, pressing the air with his palms. He looked around at Lea who stood dazed next to the car door. "Do you remember," he shouted to her, "whether there's a village?"

"I don't know where we are," she said in a small voice. With all her effort she was holding herself apart, her jaw clenched with a determination to detach herself, lifting away from the reality of what had happened and from him.

"Lea, for God's sake!" He ran his hands across the forehead of the girl, mumbling, "It will be all right. You will be all right." She looked up at him, her stern, gypsy face an eternal mask of resentment. The accusation he saw there was so overwhelming that he looked away, his eyes sweeping across the mountains, then down the road where a speeding car heading toward them had materialized.

"There's no blood," he called to Lea. "At least that. I think she might have broken something. Try to flag that car down."

"I think . . ." she began, then stopped.

"You think what?" Despising her hesitancy, her disconnection.

". . . that it is an army car, or the police."

The car was now upon them. It sped past, reversed, pulled alongside. Three officers quickly got out and asked what had happened, what they were doing there on a road in the mountains. One of them bent down to look at the girl.

"An accident," Kevin said. "I think her leg has been hurt. We must find a hospital."

They appraised him, his clothes. Approaching Lea they upheld her isolation by stopping at a respectful distance.

"Your papers?" The officiousness was startling in the quiet of the wide landscape. Kevin handed his passport case and his wallet to the thickset man, obviously senior, given the braiding on his uniform.

"And yours, madame?" Said more graciously.

Lea withdrew her pocketbook from the car and presented her passport and the automobile documents.

"You were driving?"

"No," said Kevin. "I was."

He looked at Lea. Her stillness gave no sign of having heard.

The girl had begun to hobble toward the dirt and rubble of the adjacent field.

"We try to keep them from the highways because there is always danger. They cannot be controlled." The heavy, senior officer said this, motioning one of his men to pick up the girl. It was clear that his distaste for the wretched Berber child was equal to his mistrust of these foreigners. "We will put the girl in the police car and take her to the village. But you two must come along. He will drive your car," he said, pointing to the other man. Then, to Kevin: "You will be detained."

They sat mutely in the back seat barely speaking. Kevin stared out of the window, a vein in his forehead throbbing as he clenched and unclenched his jaw. She had behaved so irrationally, driving as though deranged, incapable of helping him. And never acknowledging, even by a glance, a touch, that he'd taken the blame on himself.

With the sudden sound of snapping dogs the officers' own language bit into the air of the hills. With the child wedged between them in the front seat they had begun to amuse themselves by studying the passports, the traveler's checks and the two airline tickets in Kevin's wallet, passing them back and forth, the sound of the riffling pages not quite concealing the larger question of how these foreigners might be used.

When they reached the village it was dark. The child, now docile, was carried into a small fluorescent-lit clinic. A group of robed figures gathered at the doorway.

"There is no need for you to wait here. She will be attended to," said the officer. "But you can go," he added, to Lea. "Go back to Marrakesh in your rented car. You will have to find more money. The traveler's checks you have here will never be enough. Anyway, we must wait and see how serious the girl's condition is. This man's papers will have to be checked. And we will look into the matter in the morning."

They stood there dumbly, helpless in this web of circumstance. "Come along," the man said, ushering them into a rambling building and up some stairs. "You can sleep in there," he said to Kevin, indicating a cell-like room down a long passage. "It is not exactly a prison," he added, laughing. "It's a repository for the occasional situation like this— hitchhikers, lost hippies, foreigners whose cars break down." His laughter, his footsteps echoed behind him.

Kevin limped over to the frayed straw pallet. "I hadn't thought . . . I hadn't imagined . . . when we came to Morocco . . ." But the sentences remained incomplete. Searching in his pocket for a match, he managed to light the small kerosene lamp, though his hands shook. "I must stop this," he said half aloud. But he felt cold and he continued to shiver. "I know we'll need more money than we have. You'll find my checkbook on the bureau in the room. Call the bank first thing in the morning and tell the manager what has happened. She's a nice woman, always asking about The General. She must wire me fifteen thousand francs." He said this without looking at Lea as she stood in the shadows. "Anyway, give them the number of my account. They'll explain how it's done, how transfers are made."

"Your ankle," she said. "Can't I . . ." She moved toward him, bent down, and gently removed his moccasin. "It's swollen."

The two of them there discussing money matters. Her solicitousness. It might have been a warming, domestic scene. If only. "No, it's better not to touch it." He put his shoe back on. "I can still walk well enough to take you to the car."

In the dark street he stared at her. As though the accident had by some sorcery transposed itself through the air to fasten on her, Lea herself seemed bruised, her hair disheveled, the mauve dress frayed; beyond was the parched, moonlit landscape, land of spells and potions, of djinns that lurked behind rocks. She was disintegrating in front of him.

"Are you sure you can manage this?" he said, resenting the crispness of the sound.

She nodded.

"Well, then you might as well leave now. I guess you can get there without me," he said.

"I wonder, Kevin, if I can."

"What do you mean?" he asked, but the sound of the motor drowned out his voice.

He watched as the taillights of the car turned in a wide circle and then diminished, became tiny points of light in the darkness. Then he walked back to the building in the icy silence of the night air, limping, shivering with the cold. His eyes sought the mountain, so benign under the moonlight: the Atlas, heaved up in primeval times to keep the desert at bay. Beyond it lay the Sahara. He tried to imagine the sand under his fingers, tried to imagine running his hand across its eternity. Nothing troubled it but the wind. History did not count there, his history least of all.

Now in this rambling municipal building crafted out of baked earth he was seated on a pallet waiting to manage to sleep. The worst part was that he had already begun to miss her.

In the morning, as they inquired about him and investigated what to do with him once the money arrived, Kevin left the building unshaven, blinking in the sunlight as though he had endured a long imprisonment. He walked through the narrow streets to the high wall and out through the Saracen arch to the surrounding fields. His only aim now was to free himself from the sense of claustrophobia with which he had awakened.

His walk was noted. The women talked of him in high, chirpy voices, their veils muffling the sound. The men whose fierce country faces were lined by sun and labor, savage even while adolescent, stopped talking at his approach. He did not know whether he was well received, for here everything was ruled by concealment. He was merely fixed upon, like a target. When he stopped at the clinic to ask about the girl, he was greeted cautiously and surrounded by children who had sprouted from adjacent alleyways to observe him and comment. Limping down the road he felt rawboned and foolish, yet unashamed of being so alien to it all. He recalled his feeling as a child, that fate might have sent him to play life's game lost in the outfield where the taller grasses and the wildflowers grew, untrammeled by the more vivid players as they scudded around and around the field: Kevin Korlov, planted way beyond the sound of the grandstand. While the innings flew by, the day darkened, and no one noticed where he had gone.

The mean alleys, the high, sudden walls surrounded him. Attenuated music meandered out of the windows, melancholy laments drifting off, suddenly to be replaced by crackling static, as aggressive as an army advancing across barren plains. Inside the shadows he edged his way past the flapping laundry, the smells of things decomposing, of unknown spices; the flies gathering around the small, neat pyramids of sweets and around the rusting drains and dripping meats. The flawlessness of the morning sky as he emerged out of the archway was thrilling, the illumination dazzling him as he crossed the rotting bridge and gained the surrounding fields.

There he looked at the whole village strung along the face of the mountain, a frieze left out in the sun to dry. The river in front of it had run dry, and the massive walls, built to protect, were crumbling and neglected, with no invasion to resist.

Now in the fields Kevin was alone. He lay on his back in the small clearing between cactus and thistles, and tried, as he had been doing since the night before, to allow the surrounding calm to teach him something. On all sides of him the dry earth stretched, interrupted here and there by small groves of olive and cork trees. Way in the distance a donkey crossed a wide ravine, olive wood piled high on its back, followed by a tall figure in a flowing kaftan. But if he expected to extract some hidden revelation from the harsh earth on which he was so uncomfortably stretched he was mistaken, for he heard something move abruptly nearby and he turned quickly to see a khaki blur that was transformed as he sat up into the uniformed legs of the officer, who was looking down at him with unconcealed cunning.

"*Smahli*. I was looking for you," he said. "I did not know where you had gone."

Kevin shaded his eyes and squinted up at him, smiling cautiously. His smile was not returned. "I heard that the child will be all right."

With emphasis the officer slowly and deliberately shook his head from side to side. "I was looking for you because I thought you should know that we have contacted the Mamounia and they say you are registered there."

Resisting comment, Kevin stood.

"Also, the child is not all right. In her X-ray they found that she has fractured her leg."

"I know that. I spoke with the doctor. Still, it is a relief to know it is just that."

"I know you are not a criminal," said the man in a conciliatory tone. "But you will have many, many problems because of what happened. The family has been notified. The girl is having her leg put in a cast." He paused for emphasis. "You will need money. There will be medical bills. The family and others will have to be paid. There will possibly be a lawsuit, a trial for driving recklessly. Unless, of course, some agreement can be reached."

"Ah, yes. Of course," said Kevin. How could he have expected otherwise? A small cloud of insects swarmed nearby. Glancing below them he saw some bits of stained, rotting cloth, and caked human waste. He turned back to the officer. "Money," he said, standing. Money to hand all

around. Money to pave his way home. No subtleties were
offered or needed. The morality of the bribe was not in question. Thus abstracted from the usual conceits and games it
was what it was: beyond paying for the girl's wounded leg
and for her suffering, it was a payment for being there.

"You understand?" said the officer, his eyes onyx beads.

"Some money ought to arrive this afternoon from Paris
to Marrakesh." He began to walk back to the village. "Or
tomorrow, at the latest."

"It is almost two hundred kilometers from here to Marrakesh," the man said, falling into step. "When your money
arrives I will take you there."

"I thought you might," said Kevin.

When he walked out of the bank in Marrakesh, Kevin
held the envelope containing the money. Around the corner
the officer waited in the car. "There are fifteen thousand
francs in here. It is all I have," he said. His tone, the most
authoritative in his broadcasting repertoire, tolerated no ob-
jections. Three long days had passed before Lea had managed to leave word that the transfer had been made. Incredible
days, he had to admit, when he began to feel at ease in the
village. He had begun to grow a beard. Or try to.

"It is not acceptable. Not from a gentleman who is staying at the Mamounia."

Kevin sighed heavily. "I am not a gentleman who stays
at the Mamounia. I am someone who came here for a few
days because"—and here he managed a wan laugh—"because it sounded like such a wonderful idea."

"It will not cover all the costs."

"You are mistaken," snapped Kevin. "I asked the doctor
when I went to see the girl. It will cover a lot more than the

costs." He opened the envelope, knowing that when the man saw the neat pile of money he would relinquish his prey. "And I told the doctor, who told the girl, who told her family, who must have told everyone else, exactly how much I was giving you. So I expect that you'll hand it over to them. Most of it, that is." He produced a crooked smile of victory. It was astonishing to see how easily it made its point. To be so readily perceived as the person one pretended to be: this was Lea's trick. Her skills had not been lost on him.

The officer unclasped the envelope and looked briefly inside it as Kevin glanced through the windshield. A man brushed against the car, edging his way through the traffic holding a goat tied to a rope. Turning back, Kevin noticed immediately that by some sleight of hand the envelope had already disappeared into the upholstery of the car.

"But you lack proof that the money was given to me," said the man. He struck a match, lit a cigarette, his lips curling with satisfaction. It was his trump card.

"Ah, yes. I forgot!" Now Kevin would triumph. "I am sending the doctor this"—he withdrew the bank receipt from his pocket—"to show him that the money arrived in Morocco. You made a mistake leaving me on my own in that village, to wander around, to talk, as best as I was able, and see that I was trusted."

The man blew a circle of smoke in the air. He said nothing. Sketched on his face was an equivalent smile. Of complicity? Of respect? Finally, he nodded.

"Well, then, I must go back to my hotel." Kevin opened the car door.

"But I will drive you there." In a lofty, sweeping arc, the officer's hands lifted from the steering wheel, as though serving up the bounty of Morocco.

"I'd prefer to walk," said Kevin, removing himself from the car.

. . .

Lea was not in the room. There was only the scent of her perfume *(Mille,* he remembered, so suitable: a thousand phantom Leas). He recalled the anxiety overtaking him several days before as the sun set behind the massive Atlas, turning to her in the car, bleating for reassurance. Yet even now, without his consent, she had regained him. He wanted to hear her voice, even though she would say anything to avoid talking of love. But if she was not in the room, neither was she at the pool. In a sweat at the front desk he watched as the concierge shrugged: Possibly she was no longer in the hotel. Or in Morocco.

Back in the room he closed his eyes, recalling his yoga course, and tried pulling himself into an approximation of the lotus position, but the lingering pain in his ankle bore down on him and he abandoned it. Then he removed his glasses and lay back on the floor, rubbing his eyes. Immediately overcome by fatigue he fell into a deep sleep. It was this sprawled half-naked figure that Lea came upon when she opened the door to the room.

She did not awaken him. For a moment she stood there, staring down at Kevin, so vulnerable against the room's patterned carpeting that tears sprang to her eyes. *Maktub,* she learned, is what the Arabs say: it is written. It was written that her destiny was always to move on, to go elsewhere.

In the room the shutters were closed, and only the thinnest strips of sunlight were drawn across his body. The Invisible Man. How impossible it seemed that he could ever have thought this. This was the man who had said to the officers, *"No. I was driving,"* with such assurance, aware of all the possible consequences. He had said it to protect her while she had stood there, away from the car, eternally unable to face distress, always turning away from the wreckage left behind, the essentials. How much stronger he was than she. As she knelt down to smooth his thinning hair, he awakened with a start.

"You look well with a beard," she said, caught off guard, her hands instinctively brushing the tears from her eyes. Standing, she said, "Well, it all worked out, thanks to you."

"Lea. Oh, God, I thought I'd lost you." He reached for his glasses.

She was radiant in a white linen suit and a wide-brimmed straw hat.

"The girl fractured her leg," he said. "We were all very lucky."

"I know. They told me when I finally got through to say the money arrived."

"I did miss you," he said.

But when he went to hold her, she drew away.

"Oh, there is so much to say. So much, and yet nothing. You have had a difficult time, I know." Her mouth turned down, mimicking distress.

"The worst part was when you left."

"I would have thought it was a relief. I fell so completely apart that I was unable to help. You were a hero. I told you how you always underestimate yourself." She hugged him for his heroism and moved over to open the shutters.

He understood it all, then, in the way she had held him, in that brief, neutral embrace. He had lost her. She had removed herself from him, had inserted him into the disorder of her past. For reasons he could not understand, Lea had once again vanished. A fury suddenly rose in him for the way she looked, the way she was acting, for being left by her.

"A hero," he repeated with a wry laugh.

"Well, *I* certainly think so. You took all the bl—"

"The terrifying thing about you, Lea, is that you're not a person. You're a crowd. You insist on being one thing, then another." He waited, though she did not stop him. "The woman I fell in love with would have been here waiting to welcome me back with a decent amount of feeling, or sympathy, or whatever it's called that people are supposed to give each other, instead of all this tra-la-la."

"Certainly not! I don't want to dwell on the misery of what happened. I want us both to forget about it."

"You would say that." He stared at her suit, her hat. "Meanwhile, you seem to have flourished."

"I've arranged to replace the money you've had sent," she said, sitting on the chair. Then she removed her hat and ruffled her hair. "If that's what you're implying. I've already called Edgar about it. It will be in your bank within a week."

"Did he also send a check to the Galeries Lafayette to pay for the silk shirt you lifted for my birthday?" He was being foul, but there was no way to stop himself. "Or are you inventing Edgar's contribution the same way you invented nearly drowning off the coast of Brittany? I've listened to your fantasies, I've even enjoyed some of them. But none of them are the reason I've fallen in love with you. That person is the one you're constantly disowning. Look at you now! Listen to yourself! You've made her disappear."

"Made her become invisible." She almost laughed. "The way you were, at the beginning."

"Then we're even." He waited. "You're leaving, aren't you?" he said finally.

"Yes."

The silence was merciless. Within it they could hear birds, they could hear murmured conversations coming from the pool. They might have been able to have heard their own heartbeats.

"You're leaving me to punish me," he said, "for asking too much."

"Kevin," she pleaded, "I don't want to talk about all this. If I'm punishing anyone, it is myself. For not being able to give enough." The seriousness blocked his rage.

"Would you like to tell me where you are going?"

"No. Only because you will not believe me. And you already seem to be acquiring a list of things that you don't believe."

"Then maybe you can tell me why. Or is the question too personal, too intimate?"

She hesitated. "Oh look, Kevin. We aren't meant for each other in any way. For all my cleverness, I'm a completely frivolous woman. You must have figured that out. You seem to have discovered my secret. I live entirely in fantasy. We've had a —"

"A wonderful time."

"Yes. And as I tried to tell you in the car, it's gone wrong because it's become serious."

"For me, of course. Not for you."

She looked away from him. "I would like to say that, but I can't. I don't know all the reasons. I don't want to know. However"—she threw her hands in the air, stood, and walked to the mirror, replacing her hat—"it doesn't matter."

"It matters very much," he said. "You have no sense of the reality of what you have done. Of the consequences."

"To you," she corrected, moving toward the door. "Of what I have done to you. And I don't want to do any more." Her hand was on the doorknob.

He turned away from her, searching the room for something she might have left, the mauve dress, anything, that might mean that she would stay. But there was nothing.

"You're going on without me," he said.

"It's the same for both of us. It's also you, Kevin," she

said, "who will go on without me." She opened the door and briefly stood there, her back to him. Then she turned. "I'll write you a long letter. Or telephone from . . . from wherever I am. Or just appear one day, hoping you will still want to see me."

"I should love it above all things," he said.

15

. . . . . .

In Paris, on the warm spring days that have fastened to the city its permanent mythology, it would be an act of desecration not to allow hope into your heart. No one is expected to remain untouched, and even the dying are supposed to feel—if not hopeful, then protected; to feel that Paris's softest imaginable daylight or its most heavenly of breezes at night will accompany their transition to the Elysian fields, that other Champs Elysées.

And yet for most, life goes on in the most ordinary way. Despite the perfection of the place there are, for some, the stark truths that continue to nag. Even though it is May, even though it is Paris, even though one might still be rather young, and vulnerable, and prone to the eternal hope it proposes.

Kevin stood in the library craned over a dictionary. *Redimensionare:* an odd word, he discovered, falling somewhere between *realign, reassess, reappraise, reorganize,* and *remeasure* (from Gr. *dia* 'throughout,' plus *mene* 'moon,' becoming Lat. *mensus* 'a month'; 'a month' becoming *metiri* 'to measure,' becoming *dimetiri* 'to measure thoroughly.'

Add to this the reassuring prefix *re:* 'to measure thoroughly again.'

He had meant so often to ask Lea why she had said this was her favorite word. And now he saw it as her secret code: beginning again, each time again. Remeasuring, redimensioning her life. She had so often indicated that she wished to live this way, to avoid her true destiny, to throw it off her track.

He had tried to find her and in some ways was trying still, though he alone knew it. But he also knew that soon it would subside, that its death throes would end after a while. At the airport, when he left Marrakesh, he had found himself questioning the sly fellow behind the Royal Air Maroc counter. Had a woman—and here he listed Lea's specific attributes, described her linen suit, and, of course, her hat— had she possibly checked in on a flight that day? But the clerk merely shrugged in a world-weary way. So many flights going to so many places. And so many passengers. Too bad about the wasted ticket back, but perhaps he could get it refunded, *insh'Allah,* in Paris? You say she was a woman with a wide-brimmed straw hat? No, not that he could remember. So many women, many of them models, he'd noted, an erotic memory creasing his eyes and bringing a smile. Why concern yourself if one of them, who was not your wife, slipped off the edge of the earth? So many replacements.

Kevin obeyed the insistent announcement to board the plane and soon he had left Morocco behind him, an experience unresolved. But it was not Marrakesh that he kept remembering, it was the hills. And the idea of the Sahara beyond. Tucked away in his wallet was the extra ticket in Lea's name, her siren song humming in his ear as they flew across the southern tongue of Spain and then above the glittering Mediterranean.

In Paris he brooded about the money the trip had cost him, submerging his already diminished account to some dark and murky area where the rank cave of anxiety echoed. However, he quickly learned that a deposit had been made to cover the bank draft sent to Morocco. Perhaps he would use some of it to return there, to go deeper into the Atlas, though not just yet.

Was it possible that he might never be able to rid himself of her?

The days passed slowly. Soon it would be summer, soon the hot beaches would summon everyone south. Soon he would have cleared his mind and would join the rest of humanity, those folks who laugh and drink wine and sleep with each other with such abandon and pleasure.

If it was true that Lea had arrived in his life to tutor him on imagination, he had certainly learned his lesson. His fantasies were filled with idyllic scenes, vengeful scenes, scenes during which they tearfully reunited and static scenes showing only their bodies lying poisoned, side by side on a marble floor (the answerable goblets on a baroque table nearby). He tried to take a detached view, knowing that to be so continually obsessed would render him incapable of beginning again. There was also a practical consideration. Now that he had returned to Paris the possibility of finding her had become even more remote. She had always so successfully covered her tracks that he had almost nothing to go on. He had never even learned her precise address on the rue Boissy d'Anglas, so it was pointless to scan the uppermost windows trying to figure out which one might be hers. He had never known, anyway, whether she faced the street. Besides, it was too nineteenth century, too retro, to stand in the shade of a street lantern watching for a light on the top floor, waiting to see whether a familiar face would move toward the window to look at the night sky before pulling the curtains closed . . .

And so following his return, after picking up his dog from Mrs. Bomwalla, after picking up the pieces of the two jobs he'd almost lost because of his Moroccan caper, he spent his time trying to reconnect to what had gone before. But the detective within him persisted, spyglass in hand. He had not read all those Agatha Christie novels and stories without learning something. The mystery had to be resolved, and during one of the more aimless days, almost by chance, he found himself walking on the rue des Acacias. No name appeared on the panel, he now noticed. There he rang the same bell he had rung with freesias and hope on a recent spring night, and there he waited. From afar he heard his own ringing, and the sound of dark and empty rooms echoed ominously.

Nor was there in residence a concierge. A Portuguese maid mopping the elegant staircase put her work aside and came toward him.

"The woman who lives here," he asked. "Have you seen her?"

"The woman?"

"Yes, a young woman who is renovating the apartment."

"Gone. They have gone. Is sold."

"Yes, yes." He tried to retain his patience. "Yes, the young woman who bought it. It was sold to a young woman. I am looking for that young woman."

"No."

There was a silence. They were not understanding each other.

"Is sold. They leave. First her, maybe two months ago, six weeks. Some furniture she takes. Then him. He goes and now all the furniture gone, all of it. I have the key."

The key, the key, the key. Please, anything. Let me go in to see for myself! It has cost me so much already. The Porthault sheets, he thought irrationally, did they go when the furniture went? His memory of the sheets that he never had seen: on her bed with the sunlight streaming across them as they lay there planning their life together. He had imagined it all, forgetting that it was he who was supposed to have so little imagination. He held the key in his hand. And paid up once again.

The maid left him to walk the empty rooms while she labored on, ascending step by step as she mopped.

Aside from several frail bands of daylight the apartment was night-dark. Nothing happened when he fumbled for the wall switch in the vestibule.

"The electricity cut," shouted the maid over her shoulder, having heard the useless click.

Out of nowhere a cat bounded past him from the outside corridor and rushed on ahead through the rooms as though possessed. He walked over to the probable position of the windows and threw open a shutter that banged, violating the silence of the room.

The shrouded furniture was gone, as were the shrouds. Gone, too, was the candlelight, the piano; gone were the goblets. In the emptiness he stood at the room's edge, as though viewing a lifeless tableau. He could have been standing in a funeral parlor. The image would have pleased Lea, who was so fascinated by death. Above the fireplace a large mirror, coated with dust, gave back no reflections.

When he returned the key to the Portuguese maid, she said, "New people coming now. A family."

He said carefully, enunciating very clearly, "Are you saying that a family is moving in?"

She shook her head yes.

"And, before, it was a man and a lady?"

She said yes.

"And that the man left this week, but that the lady left—"

"Five months ago, maybe six. Wife."

Oh, God, this can't be happening. "A wife?" he repeated.

But when Kevin turned to leave (now nothing more than a homeless stray: hangdog look, tail between his legs, slinking away) she added, "Chinese."

"Chinese?"

She nodded, leaning against her mop. "Husband British man. Wife Chinese."

How the word sang through the corridor. Choruses of Chinese ladies bowed to him smiling in that way of theirs. He uncurved himself, straightened up. His step was light as he walked down the rue des Acacias.

He did not know for certain who the man and the lady were, but he did know that the lady was not Lea.

In the Métro giant posters proclaimed, "Dial SOPHIA. You do not have to be alone. Fast Action with ALPHA. Guys Meet Guys on ZIZI. Quick Sex with OMO. Your Dreams Will Be Fulfilled by GILDA." The city had gone Minitel mad. It was a wonder anyone walked into cafés with a hopeful heart when so many meetings were taking place in front of the little machines. Who could resist them?

Now it was night. The balmiest of nights. Kevin found himself seated before the illuminated screen, concentrating, staring dubiously at the possibilities offered, realities denied. He looked down. At his feet lay The General, asleep in his basket, twitching vigorously (dreaming, Kevin wondered, of battles won and decorations received?). The scene depressed Kevin: on a May evening in Paris an American man living near St. Germain des Prés, where the heartbeat of the city is at its most vibrant and hopeful, ought not to be occupied in this way. It was loathsome to be looking on the Minitel for a sign, a trace of a person who had been misplaced. Not that he expected to find her, not that he knew what would happen if he did. What she had come to represent to him had become more important than Lea herself. But he had lost her as carelessly as a piece of luggage, and he was justified in reading this computerized list ranging from aspiring romantics to insane lechers in the hope that . . . that what?

NIGHT FLIGHT immediately sent a message to THE INVISIBLE MAN: "We were wondering where you had been."

"I have been," wrote Kevin, typing rapidly and with errors, "awry, azay, away. And I am back trying to find someone here, on this list. Your memory is remarkable. You seem to know all of us very well."

The reply was almost immediate. "I am quite well informed."

"Then please, please call me. I have some things to ask you."

"This is highly irregular. I keep track of all of this only for my own amusement."

"But it is urgent," wrote Kevin. "This is not for fun."

"Once," wrote NIGHT FLIGHT, "someone's pseudo was SUICIDE, and they, too, were in trouble. But the telephone number they gave me was false. Another time someone's pseudo was I HAVE KILLED TONIGHT. Try to imagine how distraught it made everyone feel! He or she only remained on the screen for a short while. But the residue left by this announcement considerably altered the goings-on. Give me your number."

Kevin typed out his number. His telephone rang almost immediately.

"How can I help you?" The voice was deep, though

disturbingly without gender, its plangent tones reverberating around the walls of the apartment in an unearthly way.

"I appreciate you calling," said Kevin trying to keep the agitation out of his voice. "I realize that we are strangers to each other."

"That is the point."

"I am trying to discover whether a woman might have recently used this, ah, service, who has given herself, to my knowledge, two names. One is Trésors de Tendresse, and the other is Femme sous Soie."

"This will only take a minute," said NIGHT FLIGHT. "I have put all the pseudos into my personal computer. Each night I am on board, so to speak, compiling my notes. It is my passion. Ah, yes. There are seventy-four Trésors de Tendresse in France, nineteen of them outside of Paris. On this particular channel, that is. There are, as you might know, thirty-nine channels for members of the opposite sex to meet. Then there are the fifteen others for boys and boys, girls and girls, and the various combinations of the more uncertain. It is, as you probably have figured out, rather the way it is in the real world."

"Seventy-four?" repeated Kevin.

"The pseudo is not uncommon. Many women choose it, spontaneously, without intending to copy one another. Your Woman under Silk is more specialized, however. There are only thirty-one of them on my list in all of France, and two Men under Silk as well. I presume that you made the mistake of allowing yourself to take seriously an encounter—"

"Yes, yes," said Kevin.

"You have misunderstood the meaning of the game," said NIGHT FLIGHT with great gravity. "You see, you can only survive in the universe of the Minitel by remaining outside, which is what I have done. It must be seen as though from a telescope, a miniature city of light glowing in the dark. Oh, no, you must never take it seriously. That would be against the rules of the game,'' said NIGHT FLIGHT.

''The rules might apply in your case, but not necessarily . . .''

''Yes,'' said the voice swiftly. ''And so I do not suffer from desperation, the way it seems you have. I am beyond that.'' He paused. ''Or above that, if you prefer. Look, young man (if, indeed, you are young), I cannot be of any further help. Besides, I want to get back to listen in.''

''You mean, to read, to watch,'' he corrected, still the teacher. To *imagine*. ''Well, thanks,'' said Kevin into the void.

For a long while he remained there, staring at the Minitel. Its hinged keyboard fitted so nicely into the screen; snapped closed, it became a compact plastic box, an electronic aberration. How easily it could be eliminated, ''terminated,'' he said aloud, reaching across the desk to unplug the machine from the telephone, then from the wall, thus extinguishing from that computerized little universe any further lights that might have been left within it for him.

16

· · · · · ·

Bells tolled. Hourly bells, quarterly bells, from St. Germain des Prés and St. Sulpice, and from the even nearer, smaller Notre Dame des Champs and St. François Xavier, measuring the days and weeks as the summer moved inexorably ahead, imprisoning Paris under an exceptional heat, the kind of intense incineration usually reserved for the Riviera and welcomed, in fact, along those wide shores: France, Spain, and Italy embracing the Mediterranean and availing themselves of every sunbeam, every soothing breeze. But here no breezes fluttered and even the flimsiest of curtains remained motionless. Sidewalks baked, and the paved quays along the edge of the Seine had turned themselves into jampacked grids for grilling humans. Listlessly they lay, tilted at identical angles on the hard stones, a beach against which no surf would ever lap and upon which no castles could possibly be built. The chestnut leaves along the boulevards were already sere, looking autumnal or dead depending on one's vision. And so, sizzling, Paris was all but abandoned by August.

Restaurants and cafés closed, their owners and staffs fleeing into the countryside. The shops, too, were shuttered, though mainly those not actively used by the tourists, who kept coming anyway. Great busloads of pink Germans continued to appear in Pigalle for one-day visits, their occupants, unglued from their sticky seats, removing themselves into the equally red-hot streets. Stretching noisily under the noonday sun they massed in lumps to seek out whatever sin might be available close by and quickly. The Japanese, too, neatly and with precision, navigated the corridors of the Louvre. There they diligently and symmetrically gathered around the *Mona Lisa* to wreathe her with insistent smiles. And she obligingly reflected back her sort-of smile from behind her bulletproof glass, a smile so different from theirs, gamely supporting the burden of her beguiling, lingering mystery through the nights and days of her eternal enthronement.

But it was in the newer Musée d'Orsay that out of the blue Kevin ran into Lea, or a facsimile of Lea, in the striking portrait of Madame de Loyes, done in the nineteenth century and proving beyond a doubt that maybe there was something to this reincarnation business after all. So similar was she to the real Lea that Kevin experienced a bad shock and had to turn away to give himself a minute's reprieve before resuming his study of it. Surely this was Lea in one of her guises, outfitted here in black with lace cuffs: dark hair parted in the center, face exceedingly pale, her gray eyes intensely subjecting the viewer to her wiles and ways, demanding to be noticed. The painter had lit her in such a compelling way, managing to convey images of public propriety conflicting with masked lust. Kevin noted that the painting—in the so-called *style Ingres,* by Amaury-Duval—was done in 1865. The enigmatic Madame de Loyes, it seemed, had died in 1908, giving her enough time to soar through the spirit world until finding a space to become reborn in the late forties. But, of course, all this was rubbish. If he searched long enough he might find his own likeness in some painting somewhere. By whom? he wondered, now that he thought about it. And with such abandoned musings Kevin left the museum earlier than he'd planned. It was still daylight and the crowds spilling into the rue de Bellechasse strolled with the air of enjoying a midsummer night spectacle from which Kevin managed not to feel himself excluded.

Irritating to have been faced with Lea, again. Lacking even one picture of her—for they hadn't thought to take a camera to Marrakesh—should he return and photograph the painting? Surely not. What was the use? Actually, he had managed these past months to reduce Lea's size and importance in his life. She was simply there, traveling lightly within him; each day (if he had bothered taking measurements) she had become less, and soon, he believed, she would be scarcely more weighty than a cinder.

But now this portrait. Why not do his own portrait of Lea? he thought.

With grim resolve he took the bus up to the Porte des Lilas and scanned his half-finished bronzes and his tools. He put everything into crates. Then, because he knew he really had to make the effort, if only just to find out for certain, sighing heavily he removed the tools, prepared the wax, and sat perched on his stool, staring into space.

But the Lea he had expected to extract from thin air did not materialize. Perhaps she had caused him too much pain. Perhaps he no longer loved her. Perhaps she had never existed.

Throughout two of the summer's hottest weeks he sat in his studio and tried to re-create her, sweating, punishing her, punishing himself. But there was no resemblance. There was no artistry. There was no use. She remained as elusive as she had been in life. And the process itself no longer interested him anyway. Perhaps this knowledge was her final gift to Kevin-the-Artist. He had a better time teaching his students about conjunctives, broadcasting on the radio, scribbling away at translations. Thus Lea, of all people—her distorted likeness in black wax, that is—saw the last of Kevin's efforts at art. At least for then.

In a kind of euphoria of being done with his artist label, Kevin returned the key to the building's owner, a crone, shawled even in the heat, who was pleased to hear that her tenant intended to break his lease and allow her to raise the rent. She did not admit this, however. Instead, complaining and muttering she went through her ledgers meaning to extract obscure payments and make legal difficulties. Standing firm in his T-shirt and jeans, Kevin threatened and invoked, the near darkness of her dilapidated rooms surrounding them like a witch's lair, the shabby, venal dialogue lasting until nightfall.

Now officially freed from earlier dreams of creativity, Kevin went to the Worldwide Language Center and arranged to teach an additional course in the fall, at the same time letting it be known that he would also accept translation work for longer manuscripts both technical and literary. He did all of this in a straightforward manner, wound up by some higher, disciplined self who had required him once and for all to give up his toys and his illusions and behave like an adult.

His life, so shaken during the spring and so distraught in the aftermath, felt somewhat balanced.

For now he was simply Kevin-who-lived-in-Paris, who made a decent wage, who had some friends, a pleasant apartment, a companionable though woefully senior dog; who went to the dry cleaners, the supermarket; who took walks and contemplated small journeys, who was, these days, relatively open to things. Having been so dramatically set in motion, his imagination now prompted some reasonably possible personal fantasies and experiences. Had he asked himself whether his life still lacked resonance, he might have answered that it did not. However, it was a question that did not come into his head, for he had achieved a certain amount of inexplicable calm, though all of this was shattered when he arrived home one morning from his radio broadcast.

It was another of those attenuated days, with no respite from the heat, its molten hours flowing relentlessly into each other. And what happened is that he opened the door to find The General at his usual greeting post, though unable to move. Only his thin tail managed to tap out a frail, rhythmic tattoo, and when Kevin picked him up, the dog buried his gray, threadbare nose into the crook of his elbow, and there, sheltered by Kevin—who now found himself crouching near the floor muttering encouraging sounds—managed only a long, weary sigh. Holding him in this way, Kevin quickly stood, turned to rush back down the stairs (the vet, of course, would be away on vacation), but realized as he fumbled with the keys in his free hand that the creature in his arms had no breath left.

The finality of it stung Kevin, for it was not just the death of The General—though that was part of it. It was the whole time, from February's chilly, truncated days of unyielding solitude until now, when it seemed that he had found a more manageable way to get on with his life. In truth only the dog witnessed this inconsiderable transformation. There were no other allies.

He thought of this one evening later that week, in bed, rereading his Homer while battling the heat by pulling the

thin sheet over his body and then thrusting it away from him.
He was startled to realize that it was clearly Lea who had

> bent to tie her beautiful sandals on,
> ambrosial, golden, that carry her over water
> or over endless land on the wings of the wind.

He pondered it now without excessive regret. What had
it meant, her coming to him, flashing down from outer space
only to have left without even a kiss goodbye?

It was this question that was darting in and out of his
consciousness the evening he encountered Edgar crossing to
the Ile de la Cité on the Pont Notre Dame. But at first he
hadn't known who the man was; it seemed to be someone
from India coming toward him unshaven, with an open smile.

"Aha!" said the man with a delighted air, extending his
hand toward Kevin. "You don't recognize me."

"Frankly, I . . ." He studied the man: greasy black hair,
dark-skinned, tall, slightly stooped as though in apology.

"Edgar," said the man.

"Edgar? Well . . ." There was an instant of hesitation.
Then certain features fell into place. "What a surprise. I
hadn't quite . . ."

"No, I'm not looking very well," he said. "I've been in
prison. I've only just got out."

Kevin opened his mouth and could find nothing to say.

"I have a tale to tell," said Edgar, his voice transposed
into a surer key as he straightened up, motioning them toward a café near the bridge. His walk was now brisk, and
somehow British.

"The fact is," he said after they were seated and had
ordered drinks, "for three weeks I've been posing as an Indian. It wasn't difficult, as you can see. I got myself a fine
suntan in Cannes, practiced the proper accent, and have been

walking around Paris with papers that are not quite in order, false identification papers arranged for me by my newspaper.''

''Yes,'' agreed Kevin, ''you succeed. In looking the part, I mean.''

''Exactly. Like almost everyone else I am at heart an actor. So as I expected, I was picked up by the police. Not for doing anything wrong, mind you. Just for having the wrong skin color and looking a bit shabby. Look, it's a longish story, and I'm not sure—''

''For Christ's sake, Edgar, of course I'm interested. This happened here? In Paris?'' Acutely conscious, once again with Edgar, of his own tenuous connection to commitment, his political superfluousness.

''France! Its racism is not generally known by the outside world, which prefers images of Château d'Yquem and bound volumes of Proust. And as they pick up about a hundred people a day and heave them into jail because their dark skin makes them suspicious and might mean trouble, I was treated, as an Indian, to one of their more uncelebrated accomplishments. It's the *other* France. Each country has one.''

The waiter approached the table, setting down the drinks without comment.

''Anyway, I was kept for thirty-six hours without being able to call anyone. And then I was only allowed one call. That is routine. Had I a family or friends, they would have thought that I'd simply been run over or thrown into a back alley. I was kept in a cell with twenty others and I slept on the floor. The guards had a good time knocking us all around: the Senegalese, the Arabs, and so on. You'll read it in the article. I got an elbow in my back and spent three days vomiting blood, so this wreck you see is not all a disguise. It makes your American South look like the promised land. Well . . .'' He sighed heavily. ''What is perhaps *worse* is that after the thing is published no one will pay very much attention to it anyway, and as you say in the States, that's the way it goes. All in a day's work. Oh, by the way,'' he added, ''have you heard from our friend?''

There was a pause. Kevin cleared his throat, looked at the wavering amber of his whiskey and swallowed it down. He knew that it was now, after his raging uncertainty, that he would sit there in this café and listen to it all tumble out across the table, as casually as a handful of pick-up-sticks. He also knew that it made hardly any difference to him, realizing it with a sudden, awful sadness. He felt Edgar staring at him, Lea's old, dear friend (*A friend in need is a friend indeed*—remember to put in the commas). He shook his head. ''I've lost her,'' he said finally.

Edgar smiled. ''Oh, she's an evasive one all right.''

''I don't mean only that I've lost her in space. Lost, you know, like in something no longer possessed. I must tell you, in the time we were together I never managed to understand her.''

''Of course, isn't that the point with Lea?'' said Edgar, signaling the waiter for another round. ''To *not* understand? That's why I love her. My entire life is dedicated to understanding everything, all the time. To being relentlessly factual. And here's this beautiful creature who absolutely denies facts. I mean, she works the truth over until it becomes what one might call dream wishes. She changes the way she looks. She changes cities. She changes lives. Her own and the lives of the people she is close to, if only for a while. I always find it such a relief to be with her, though admittedly her gift for fantasy might not be everybody's cup of tea. How she made me laugh, when I was living on the rue des Acacias.''

''I wanted to ask you about that,'' said Kevin. Now the plunge had been taken. Icy waters. He sipped the remainder of his drink to warm himself. ''She had told me that it was her apartment. That she was fixing it up. I went back there and it was empty.''

''Ah, yes. Sad, sad. My wife and I lived there until our divorce. Then I stayed on alone, and finally it was too much. I was getting ready to move out just around the time that you paid us a visit.''

''Then it was your apartment. And your wife—was she . . . Oriental?''

''Yes, Japanese,'' said Edgar casually. Then, ''Well, you see in a way it *was* Lea's apartment. When I was out of town on assignments, Lea house-sat. Sometimes she stayed there with me, just because it was pleasant for both of us. You see, all her stories have a grain or two of truth. Her own, modest apartment was that tiny place she called a rathole, on the Boissy d'Anglas.''

''I never saw it. Her life remained very private.'' Kevin's voice trailed off, nursing these reopened wounds.

''I'm not surprised. She wasn't very proud of it. It's what they call in the States a cold-water flat and it had bad memories. In a way, it exposed her defeat. When she grew up she had such conspicuous promise that she must have expected that anything, everything was possible. She is really quite brilliant, you know, though completely unsure of her abilities. I remember visiting her there as she sat in her bathtub (which was really a large sink, installed at floor level). She'd answered the door in her robe, always so beautiful, so damn *decorative*. She invited me in, removed the robe and resubmerged herself in the tub—our relationship, you ought to know, was never anything but friendship. So she sat there doing her nails, chatting away about new plans, new hopes, saying that maybe she'd try for a film career, knowing all the while how impossible it would be. She made it all sound so amusing, fanning out her fingers and studying them, all newly polished. And the next night she tried to take her life.''

"Christ! I knew it. She told me she'd almost died in Brittany. Or was it Normandy? And didn't say it was suicide."

Edgar nodded, slowly revolving his glass. "She had a right to that, I suppose."

They looked away from each other.

"It seems unfair to talk about her when she's not here," said Kevin.

"I guess I've always given her too many rights, spoiled her," said Edgar, as though to himself. "Unfair? No. I'm too much of a journalist, and it seems to me that you have a a right to know all this along with the rest. She tried to kill herself by taking an overdose of sleeping pills because she knew she was running out of the thing that sustained her the most, her belief that anything was possible. It wasn't pretty stuff, I assure you, with all that pumping machinery and Lea splayed out like a rubber doll, the neighbors clustered around the staircase asking whether she was dead. So our Lea was required, by circumstance, to live. Living for her, from then on, occurred on another plane where nothing was allowed to touch or threaten her. It wasn't Brittany or Normandy or anything windswept and romantic. She changed it a bit, made it prettier. But the essence is the same. That's the way with most of her stories. Her father was a functionary in the diplomatic corps but she prefers to remember it differently. She has a very small income from her family. The worst kind to have. A tiny income, and a vast imagination."

Kevin sighed. "I was in love with her," he said simply.

Edgar looked at him, his smile gone. "I hadn't realized that. I'm sorry. I thought you two were just—I don't know—just having a great old time together."

"I wasn't looking for an antidote to reality, to facts," said Kevin. "And unlike you, I could never have appeared as a dream prince."

"Well, to begin with, you didn't find her sprawled unconscious across a bed. And you were not the one to save her life, as it were.''

"I don't mean just that. I never realized why she became interested in me. After all, I don't ever have very much money, and I'm not," he grinned with irony, "such a great catch.''

"Listen, Kevin," Edgar reached over and shook his shoulder. "She is in many ways an extremely generous person, though it might not seem so in the usual sense. Her intuition is extraordinary. Maybe she liked you in bed, or as a friend, or maybe she saw things in you that you don't see. The question, you know, is really rather unimportant. How can we ever define what brings us together? I know she was extremely fond of you, which surely must have frightened her a good deal. Anyway, I can see from your face that it is a story that has come to its end.''

"Yes," said Kevin. "She left me in Morocco.''

"I see," said Edgar. "I guess that explains everything.''

Kevin announced, "I'm going back there. Before the new term begins.''

Edgar said quickly, "Oh, no, don't try to follow her to Africa. She is untrappable in every way. Anyway, there's no need . . .''

"No," said Kevin. "Not because I want to look for Lea. I'm going back because I never really saw it, and there were a few moments there where I thought I might be on to something.''

"Aha!" said Edgar. "A good story?''

"No, personal, I mean. I'm going to rent a Land Rover, drive across the Atlas to the Sahara.''

"Ah, lucky. Always wanted to visit the Sahara and never have." Edgar drummed his fingers on the table and contracted his considerable eyebrows. "Maybe I could take a small holiday and join you if the timing worked out. Though knowing myself as I do, I'd probably wind up doing a story on corruption in the camel market. Well, we'll see.'' He smiled. ''But, sorry, I was saying don't try to trap Lea, because I thought you meant to track her down. There's no reason to bother.''

''I guess that means you know where she is,'' said Kevin, putting down his glass very slowly. ''Where. And why.''

''I cannot tell you the why. I could never know that about Lea. As I've been saying, that was her charm for me. Never knowing.''

Kevin nodded and made the humming noises of agreement that the situation called for.

''Anyway, she's been staying on the Ivory Coast. In Abidjan. Sounds like a magic carpet ride, doesn't it? Someone is surely taking care of her. Someone always will. We both know that.''

Kevin looked down at the café table and nodded. Then he lifted his head and tried out a smile. Hunching his shoulders, he raised his arms supporting emptiness.

''Come on,'' said Edgar. ''Let me invite you to dinner.''

''Ah, no,'' said Kevin. ''The invitation's mine. And you just got out of jail.''

''All right,'' said Edgar, rising. ''That is fine. Fine. But let me go home first and get out of this disguise. I was released from jail this morning and went straight to the office without even taking a shower. I think I might have picked up some lice. You're a brave fellow to have let me sit opposite you at this small table.''

As he stood, Kevin hesitated. ''Abidjan,'' he said, trying out the unaccustomed word, its vowels and consonants knocking into each other in a mysterious way.

''Oh, the large cities on the Ivory Coast are extraordinary places, rich, thriving, filled with every imaginable race, language,'' said Edgar, digressing again, which was his habit.

"Those cities have survived everything: the decline of the rest of Africa, the disasters that leftist and fascist governments have left behind—famine, plagues. Yes, only the survivors are left. Like all of us. Like Lea until now, though like the rest of us, she's also getting a bit too old for these constant changes. I think, judging by her last letter, that she realizes she's becoming rather tired of it all. She's too smart not to know that the game can't go on forever. With all this talk about Lea, I do miss her. Not as much as you do, I suspect. But I do miss her. When I think about the material I'm always working on, being with Lea was such a vacation from it all.''

Edgar moved away as Kevin followed him down the broad quay. As they began to cross the bridge, a sudden chilly wind came off the Seine, the branches along the quay bent and swayed, signaling the possibility of an early autumn.

Over his shoulder Edgar said, "But you know, you interrupted me earlier. I was about to tell you that she is coming back to Paris. They all come back in September. All those friends of mine who think they've left Paris forever. I have a neighbor who went to Katmandu to enter an ashram. He reappeared yesterday.''

"Oh," is all Kevin could manage to say.

"They all come back from exotic places and end up, well, doing what everyone else does. I guess it's inevitable.'' He threw up his hands in mock resignation.

"She will go on from Abidjan to Xanadu. And then farther,'' Kevin continued in an unexpected monologue, "up, up, back home finally to Olympus . . .'' He stood there, lost in these images.

Because it was cold, and Edgar was tired, and he had been in jail, and as the conversation seemed to be edging toward the poetic, he took Kevin by the elbow to urge him to continue walking. "My car's parked just over there, near

the Hôtel de Ville. It's a very battered Peugeot, but it works.''
He looked at Kevin, who refused to move.

He could not move because he was immobilized by the
idea that she would return. In his determination to be rid of
her she had already perished. He had mourned, then, for all
things that die, for all hopes that remain unrealized. As
though searching for solace, Kevin looked at the rigid Gothic
towers not yet illuminated, so remote, so sane and solemn
in contrast to the hectic activity on the streets below, where
all those ordinary lives like his were crossing and converging.

"Well, at the moment you oughtn't to complain,'' said
Edgar, impatiently heading them rapidly across the bridge.
Below them the barges cut swiftly through the river.

"Yes, at the moment I have Paris,'' Kevin said, prepared
to marvel at the possibilities.

"You'll see her, I imagine,'' Edgar said.

"No. No, I won't see her.'' Now that he was finding his
road, he would go his own way.

"In my business,'' said Edgar, "very few stories have
final endings.''

It was dusk. The lanterns marking the bridge flickered
and went on. "Do you mean happy endings?'' asked Kevin.

But Edgar was a few steps in front of him and did not
answer. The evening breeze had carried away the question.

A NOTE ON THE TYPE

The text of this book was set in a digitized version of
Times Roman, a typeface designed by Stanley Morison for *The Times* (London), and first introduced by
that newspaper in 1932.

Among typographers and designers of the twenti-
eth century, Stanley Morison was a strong forming
influence, as typographical adviser to the English
Monotype Corporation, as a director of two distin-
guished English publishing houses, and as a writer of
sensibility, erudition, and keen practical sense.

Composed by Creative Graphics, Inc.,
Allentown, Pennsylvania

Printed and bound by The Haddon Craftsmen, Inc.,
Scranton, Pennsylvania

Designed by Dorothy Schmiderer Baker